RILEY HOUSE

HOLLY KNIGHTLEY
RILEY
LOUISE
KNIGHTLEY

For Bill and Beth

CONTENTS

CHAPTER ONE: *Sip Happens* 1

CHAPTER TWO: *Déjà vu'* 10

CHAPTER THREE: *The White Rabbit* 20

CHAPTER FOUR: *Life is Full of Surprises* 25

CHAPTER FIVE: *The Portrait* 28

CHAPTER SIX: *Stranger Things* 31

CHAPTER SEVEN42 *Jacklyn Riley* 42

CHAPTER EIGHT: *The Rats* 57

CHAPTER NINE: *The Confession* 65

CHAPTER TEN: *The New Beginning* 83

THE KILLING TREE: CHAPTER ONE: *The Confession* 87

CHAPTER ONE

Sip Happens

I felt lightheaded from the blood loss; sick—a wave of nausea washing over me as I fought the urge to vomit. "I can't believe this is how I'm going to die," I said over and over again as if repeating this mantra would somehow save my life. The repetition of words, at the very least, gave me something to focus on besides dying. Somehow the idea of being discovered murdered, lying in my own vomit, would make my death just that more indignant, that much harder for me to accept.

It's true what they say, when you're about to die, your life flashes before your eyes. And now, at the moment of my demise, my head was spinning like a cyclone, whipping around my memories—things I did and things I still wanted to do if only I had the time. Death by teacup—no, more precisely—death because of a stupid teacup at the age of twenty-two is a hard pill to swallow. I was up to my neck in hot water and no amount of tea whether it be herbal, green, English, hand-brewed, hard, or Arnold Palmer's would make dying this way palatable. So much for crossing off retiring with a pension from my bucket list.

The par-tea's over, it's time for the 'mad' executioner to be off with my head. Kettle down Morris, the cost for a cup of tea is a bit steep. Sip happens, you're going to die.

It amused me, at the time, to think of all the silly tea related puns I could—anything to distract myself from the imminent arrival of the Grim Reaper. But then, like always, my intuitive nature brought me back to reality with the simple question of why—but why? Why was this happening to me? When did my nearly perfect life get flushed down the rabbit hole to Hell?

* * *

It all started a few weeks ago. My perfect life became nearly perfect thanks to one decision. It was a turn in the wrong direction—a turn down a dead end. You see, my wife and I had been married for only a few weeks and were still in the honeymoon period of our relationship. I was willing to do anything to make her happy. Oh, how my friends thought I was crazy getting married in my twenties. I thought I was lucky. I got to skip all the hardships of dating and move straight to marital bliss.

From the first moment I met Liz, every cheesy romance movie cliché came true. I was in love, drowning in it, and enjoying the need to come up for mouth to mouth. Oh, what I wouldn't do for just one more rescue breath. I didn't have to be a certain age, earn a particular income, or even be finished with college to pop the big question on one knee. I just wanted to be with her forever.

Liz was my complete opposite, and I was attracted to

her like she was the world's strongest magnet. Like I said, I have a curious nature, nosy even. I have this built-in need for everything to be just right, my proverbial ducks in a row. I'm the kind of guy that always tucks his shirt in and wears a belt—yes, even on the weekends. Liz is an artist in all the ways we non-artsy people think of them—hippie-like, animal activists, and tree huggers.

Liz is everything right in the world rolled up into paint covered overalls and I'm everything wrong with the world—I'm a realtor. A damn good realtor, but still, I'm a realtor, even if it's not for much longer.

Though I was opposed to buying a fixer upper, I knew what I had to do to get the house of my wife's dreams for a steal. I wished I would've stood my ground, but Liz had me wrapped around her finger. It was the way she looked at me with those slate-gray eyes of hers, like I was the only person that mattered. She believed in me—believed that with my company pen I could move mountains.

"The price dropped on that house I really like," Liz had told me, putting her hands on the inside of my thighs and squeezing. Okay, I admit it was her eyes and the way she knew just the right place to apply the right amount of pressure. I had already known the price dropped on the house she'd been watching. The property value had depreciated but it was an opportunity to get into a good neighborhood at a bargain price. The value would go up, anyone could see that. So, like any loving real estate savvy husband, I closed the sale on the old house at the corner of Main and we became the proud owners of a borderline condemned Colonial in Keyport, New York.

This is where it all started—the plummet down the rabbit hole. Maybe I had blinders on when we walked through the house or maybe I'm just whipped, love struck—dumb, but the amount of work the house needed suddenly seemed insurmountable even at the basement bargain price we got it at.

"Just think," Liz had said, pulling on my arm, planting a kiss on my cheek, "we live on Millionaire's Corner."

Maybe, a century ago, our house situated on one of the four corners making up Millionaire's Corner was worth a fortune, but now it was going to cost a million in renovations to get it up to date within this century. Liz convinced me it was worth it to live in the historical part of town where all the houses that lined Main Street were statement pieces. Our house, like the other three homes comprising Millionaires Corner, was built by renowned architect Charles Riley, and according to Liz—and Liz alone—was his magnum opus.

What exactly is Millionaire's Corner you ask? It's the Keyporter's idiom for the four Charles Riley homes situated on the intersection of Main and Keyport Road, the only road in and out of the rural river town. Keyport is located on the fringes of the Empire State just outside the commuter purview.

My wife said we could reno one room at a time, and we would have to. Like I said, the extent of the renovation was more than I had anticipated. If that wasn't bad enough, I got stuck playing house sitter to my new neighbor's house. It was just like a Keyporter, (what the locals referred to themselves as) to entrust a stranger they'd just met with keys to their home.

The story goes like this: Our neighbor Kevin and his

wife bought their dream house by the water close to family and needed someone to make sure their realtor (not me) locked the doors when they finished showing potential homebuyers the house and check to ensure the old heater didn't kick off with winter being right around the corner.

Since I myself am a realtor, 'I would be able to keep an eye on a fellow cohort', whatever that meant. Undoubtedly, I did have the experience of using a set of keys and could be trusted with locking a door as anyone over the age of six or a member of the primate family could. I'm pretty sure my sister's cat can open doors, not sure about locking them, but I digress. I was tasked with this honor over the neighbors Kevin had known for years because they left their front door unlocked, a bad habit formed thanks to Keyport's low crime rate. In Kevin's eyes it made them untrustworthy to play house-sitter and me the only suitable candidate.

I didn't argue the point children and cats could close doors. There was no point. Kevin was already putting the keys in my shirt pocket before I could say no.

There I was, turning the key in my neighbor's front door. The looming entrance was slicked with rain that beaded over its glossy veneer. It was stuck. I jiggled it a little, putting pressure on the warped door with my shoulder. A shove. Relief. I got it open, years of mildew hitting me in the face. Thankfully, even amidst moving, I was my usual anal self and had already taken my allergy pill in the morning. I felt safeguarded from the tiny spores that were no doubt traveling up my nose as I pressed my way into the house.

Let it be officially known, I hate old houses. It didn't

matter to me the house I now stood in would have brought architects to their knees, with its twelve-foot ceilings, fancy crown molding, pocket doors, paneled walls, American stained glass, and double walnut staircase. The features of my neighbor's house were too many to count and so ornate I felt like it was overdone and frankly a little gauche.

Kevin's house was Charles Riley's very own country home, the crown jewel of his accomplishments and wealth and his *true* magnum opus. Kevin's house, also known as Riley House, was on sale when we bought our home, but thanks to the extra bells and whistles it was way out of our price range and like I said, it was too over the top for me.

Despite Riley House being a literal mansion, in every sense of the word, it was easy to do what Kevin requested of me. I could tell the heat was working just by entering the house. I felt I only needed to walk the main floor to make sure everything was as it should be, and the doors were locked. The first day Kevin gave me the keys, Liz and I spent what seemed like hours going through the rooms at Riley House. It seemed superfluous to spend another hour wandering about just to make sure my 'cohort' locked up everything on the second and third story.

Kevin and his wife had already moved what they wanted to their new house and left what they didn't want. This seemed to be everything besides a large wooden hutch in the living room. It was tightly squeezed between floor to ceiling built-in cabinets like a linebacker in the middle seat of an airplane. It was the kind of monstrosity used to display fine china. The kind of dishware my grandmother pulled out around the holidays and always washed by hand.

Standing in front of the hutch, the little hairs on the back of my neck stood up. I couldn't help myself; it was instinct. I ran my hand over the gooseflesh on the nape of my neck. I questioned if the heat had in fact kicked off, but concluded the living room was just particularly drafty, the way old houses tend to be.

I confess, however, there was something off about Riley House. It made me feel silly to think it then and now as I recall it. A house is just four walls with a roof and a floor after all. But there's a funny feeling that comes with being in an old house that's vacant, but not condemned.

You see, Riley House is not the kind of house squatters graffiti on or racoons nest in. Taking into consideration the musty smell, Riley House was tidy, sturdy, and still—like it was sleeping. There was something about the stillness there. I felt like I stepped into a void. Time around me ticked on, but while I stood as still as the house, I felt timeless or maybe I was sinking into the same sleeping spell this once magnificent house had succumbed to.

I became aware of a teacup on the floor in front of the hutch. I knelt to pick it up, the floor moaning under my weight, to which I rolled my eyes. It was the universe telling me I was packing on the pounds. I had noticed. We had been in our new home for only a week and my power pants fit tightly. It was all the eating out we'd been doing which came with the territory of not having a fully functional kitchen. It was microwave or delivery. Sure, I could have ordered a salad, but if I'm ordering out, I'm getting a cheesesteak, without the cheese—I try to eat kosher—or General Tso's chicken with fried rice and a can of Coke—not diet, the real stuff. A long run on the weekend, and a water detox would bring balance to my sudden junk food diet, and I would be back to normal.

If I had known that this seemingly innocent teacup would shatter my life and normal would become a thing I would never get back, I would've taken a sledgehammer to it right there on the spot, not stopping my assault until it was a fine powder. But instead, I sucked in my stomach and picked it up.

I hadn't noticed it on my walkthrough with Liz. It was cute—the kind you imagine rich girls of yesteryear using at a tea party. The teacup had hand painted roses around its scalloped rim. It was lighter than I'd expected. In fact, it was the most fragile teacup I had ever held. Self-possessed of delicate, fine china—bone-china. I felt like I could crumble it in my hands if I chose to.

I'd learned from my grandmother this type of fine china was made by grinding up animal bones. I always thought it was gross, and as a child would never sip out of one of her cups. But now, as an adult, I can appreciate the uncanny translucence and delicateness it gave the porcelain—it was stunning.

I'm not sure why I did what I did next. I suppose I was looking for a maker's mark, the way the antique dealers on Antique Roadshow always do, but I turned the teacup upside down. I didn't see a seal or anything that made me think the teacup was worth money but on the bottom of the teacup, painted in the same vein as the roses, it read Elizabeth Riley.

That made me smile. My wife's name is Elizabeth, though no one calls her that. She's a Liz, and that is that.

I imagined Elizabeth Riley as a little girl with blonde hair and green eyes, the child I had first suspected the teacup belonged to. I surprised myself with my attention for detail.

Liz must be rubbing off on me.

I placed the teacup on the center shelf of the hutch before I locked the front door of Riley House, pulling the doorknob to make sure the lock caught, and headed home to my nightmare.

CHAPTER TWO
Déjà vu'

The following day after work, I parked in my driveway and crossed the street to Riley House. I rubbed my hands together to keep my fingers from going numb. Halfway through my walk I decided to park at Riley House the following day and skip the short walk. It was cold for early November, and I could do without the wind chapping my hands and face even if the walk to my neighbors took less than two minutes. It would still be two minutes spared of unnecessary discomfort. I was used to city life, and the tall skyscrapers of New York City blocking the onslaught of the wind. Cold I could handle, but the sting of the wind I will never get used to.

I missed the city and our high-rise apartment. Our new house was located an hour out of the heart of NYC. I still commuted to work—drove to the train station, then took the train like millions of other commuters into the Big Apple. I had no choice. The real estate market in Keyport wasn't hot and I could never make the money I made in New York realty anywhere else. Besides, we needed to fund our money pit, and my family lived in the city.

When it came time to house hunt, Liz wanted a little more space and owing to the fact she was from Keyport, it was a natural choice to start our house hunt there. I had never heard of Keyport when she pulled up the for-sale stats on Google. Admittedly, I liked Keyport when we visited. It didn't seem as rural as other small towns and the stately architecture of downtown reminded me of the brownstones in Brooklyn. But the people were different, they were stuck in the past, like they still viewed TV on black and white televisions while the rest of the world was in color on iPhones. You would never know they were a short train ride outside of the busiest city in the world.

Without delay, I unlocked the gargantuan lacquered front door to Riley House, grateful for the heat that was still working. I made my rounds around the main floor of the house making sure no one broke in, finishing my walk-through of the living room. Like the day before, I saw the teacup on the floor in front of the hutch. I stared at it for a long while, trying to remember if I had placed it back on the floor or in the china hutch. My pulse raced under my skin like every nerve in my body was on fire. I knew I was under a lot of pressure from work and Liz, but could I really not recall what I did just the day before? There was something scary about that. I know I was anal retentive, a quality no one, not even Liz thought was endearing, but being unsure of my actions really got under my skin.

There was this nagging feeling clawing at the inside of my skull that something strange was afoot. The longer I stood in the silence of Riley House, under the waning sunlight filtering through the tall, narrow windows, the more I was certain I placed the teacup in the hutch yesterday.

This conviction only acted to unsettle me. I didn't understand why I was making such a big deal over the teacup being on the floor. It was just a silly teacup after all. I placed it back in the hutch, convincing myself it was possible I'd left it on the floor.

There was no sign of forced entry. Why would someone come and move a teacup? The idea of it sounded just as stupid then as it does now as I think about it, but I couldn't shake the strange feeling. I left no room for doubt this time. Upon placing the teacup in the hutch, dead-centered on the middle shelf, I snapped a picture on my phone. Satisfied with that, I locked up and walked home.

* * *

I thought about that bone-china teacup with its hand-painted pink roses, glazed with a glossy luster all night. All night I let it bother me. I really needed to get a life. Clearly obsessing as I did, was not normal. My wife tried to placate my temperament, listing a multitude of possibilities for the teacup being on the floor: Kevin stopping by, my cohort—the other realtor, a thirsty racoon. Ultimately, she believed a child moved it. She informed me that during the day several families, some with children, came to look at Riley House. She had watched the children play in the front yard from her art room window.

Being that Liz is a freelance artist, the first room renovated in our fixer upper was her art studio, which for my ease of mind, conveniently faced the neighbor's house. That tidbit helped me get to sleep.

* * *

For reasons not understood, I was anxious to get to Riley House the next day. I left the office early to catch an earlier train. My car drive home from the train station dragged on. A nervous energy traveled down my arms to my fingers, forcing me to tap on my steering wheel to the sound of falling rain hitting the windshield.

Putting my car in park and leaving the engine running, I made a beeline to the living room, taking only the time necessary to grope the wall for the light switch. The room came to life, a gasolier style chandelier with glass globes lit, casting shadows on the blank walls.

I fumbled for my phone, dialing my wife. "The teacup's on the ground."

"Morris, honey, just put it back on the shelf."

"Did the realtor come by today?"

"I'm not sure. I was so into my painting I didn't really notice, but if the teacup is mov—"

"It is," I interrupted, my agitation building like a steam locomotive. Why didn't she understand how much this bothered me? Why couldn't she have paid attention to the comings and goings at Riley House?! I had asked her to keep an eye on the house. I had uprooted my whole life for her, why couldn't she do this one thing for me?

Liz remained kind but firm. "Well Morey, that means someone moved it. Put it back. Make sure the windows and doors are locked and come home."

I hung up. *The windows.* I hadn't checked to make sure they were locked. How stupid could I be?! I checked all the windows in the house starting on the top floor. Yes—yes, I know this was most likely not necessary, but I didn't want to leave one stone unturned. Concluding my window check, I found two unlocked on the first floor. At first, this finding brought me peace, a little Zen in my crazy life, but that peace quickly shifted to anger at the idea of some punk kid pranking me.

I held that anger in, just in case the derelict was watching from a window. I would never know, it was pitch dark outside by the time I'd checked every window in Riley House. I wouldn't give them the pleasure; this game was over. I locked the front door and went home.

* * *

The next day I followed the same routine, parked at Riley House and sauntered into the living room expecting to see the teacup where I had placed it in the hutch. Over the phone, Liz had already confirmed no one came to Riley House that day. I felt excited, my willful need for everything to be just right would finally be met and I could go home happy.

My heart dropped when I saw the teacup was on the floor again in front of the hutch as it had been the day I first discovered it.

I called my wife. "It happened again."

"What did?"

"The teacup's on the floor. You're sure no one came into the house today?"

"No honey."

"No honey what?!" I said exasperated. "No, I'm not sure or no, no one came into the house?"

Liz breathed heavily into the phone, her voice laced with a sharpness she seldom used. "No one went into Riley House today."

"What am I supposed to do?"

"Morris, it's just a teacup," Liz said, her voice becoming a whine.

"I know that, but why is it being moved? Today it's a teacup, tomorrow they can bust out the windows. I'm the only one with a key, it will come back on me. The last thing we need is to be stuck paying for new windows for Riley House when our house needs them. I think I should file a police report."

"On a teacup?"

"On a break in," I said frustrated. "We don't need another problem."

"Okay if it will make you feel better but—"

I hung up. It *would* make me feel better.

* * *

Sitting across from Officer Randall, I felt anything but better. His response to the teacup being moved was as close to Liz's as it could be. I felt like I was the only one not in on the joke. I don't know why I thought the Keyport police would take a break in seriously.

"Was anything taken from the house?" Officer Randall asked with a voice so dry it sounded like it hurt to speak.

I steepled my hands on his desk. "No, like I said the house is empty."

"Except for the teacup?" Officer Randall asked, looking up from his lined notepad.

"Well yes, and there's a hutch too."

"Was it taken?"

I exhaled loudly. "No."

"And the teacup wasn't taken, just moved—is that correct?"

"Yes. Three days in a row someone took the teacup from the hutch and placed it on the floor."

Officer Randall gave me a look over. I'm guessing ascertaining what type of drugs I was on. "And the doors and windows were locked?"

"Yes, like I said, I have the only key." I wasn't going to tell him I forgot to check the windows until last night.

"And you said it was Kevin Riley who gave you the key. Are you sure about that?"

I didn't say exactly that—just that Kevin gave me the key. I never got a chance to ask his last name, which I was not in the practice of doing. Etiquette was a key to success in New York City. Introductions began with a firm handshake and an exchange of full names. It was just that Kevin was so assertive and in such a rush he bypassed all the normal particulars.

"Yeah, tall guy with a gray beard," I answered, adding a little description just in case the Kevin I knew wasn't Kevin Riley.

With a thinking tap to his chin, "I guess it's possible someone is breaking in and then locking up afterward. I wish all criminals were so considerate."

I was beginning to understand how stupid I sounded. If I hadn't hung up on Liz, I'm sure she would've talked me out of doing this. "I know I sound stupid." What else could I say at this point? I was the village idiot.

The officer tried to hold back a grin. He was a younger guy about my age. I was grateful he was young and not an old-timer. I figured someone with more experience wouldn't have even entertained my police report.

I suddenly felt the need to justify my coming to the police station. "Listen, I'm new to Keyport and I just don't want any trouble. I don't want someone to thin—"

Officer Randall finished my sentence. "Think you moved a teacup."

My face flushed. I was sure I looked every bit as red as a Jersey tomato, the kind genetically modified at a lab to be brighter than red and shipped to New Yorkers for a taste of the Garden State. "Yeah that. And I was worried it was a teacup today and broken windows tomorrow. I'm sure the locals know the house is vacant. A vacant house is a green light for vandals. I would know, I'm a realtor. I just didn't want this coming back on my wife and me."

Officer Randall tapped on his notepad. "As you know you have to pass Millionaire's Corner to get in and out of our little town. Everyone here knows of Riley House; it would be silly for anyone to vandalize it." He stared at me as if he wanted to say something else, but concluded with, "I wrote down your complaint of a possible break in, so if things escalate, we have it on paper you came forth. I'll make sure to drive past Riley House at the end of my shift and check the windows and doors."

"Thank you officer," I said, trying to sound grateful, knowing I wasn't the best actor. I was the kind of kid that got pushed to stage crew when it came time for the school plays.

"One more thing," Officer Randall said as I made my way to the door. "Is the teacup worth anything?"

I shrugged. I had no clue. "It's old," I offered. "I'm not sure how much an old teacup is worth, if anything."

"Nothing for nothing Morris. It's Morris, right?"

"Uh yeah, Morris. Morris Rossman," I said, annoyed he'd already forgotten my name.

"Well Morris, if the teacup is really bothering you why don't you just take it home. Keep it at your place until the next time Kevin comes into town. If it's not in the house, no one can move it, and if someone is messing with you, well shoot, you just went and spoiled their fun."

I felt even stupider if that was possible. Of course, I should take the teacup home. If I remove the source, the game is over. I went in for a handshake. "Thank you," I said again, this time meaning it.

I went straight to Riley House after the police station. The door was really stuck. I felt like a battering ram getting it open. I was not surprised to see the teacup on the ground but was happy to know this would never happen again with the teacup at my house.

Like Riley House, our little money pit had a large china cabinet left to us by the last owners. It was bulky and dark, taking up the entire wall in our living room. I hated it and my partner in crime, Liz, loved it. She said it gave the room character. I wasn't sure about that, but it did cover up the mold growing on the wallpaper directly behind it.

And now it would hold the Elizabeth Riley teacup. I opened the center door to our hutch and placed the teacup behind the glass.

CHAPTER THREE
The White Rabbit

The next morning I went downstairs feeling refreshed. I slept better than I had since we moved in. I made my way into the living room to stare at the face of my triumph. My heart jumped, sweat beaded in my palms, the teacup was not where I placed it. I heard Liz humming in the kitchen, I ran to tell her about the missing teacup.

Liz was already asleep by the time I got back from the police station. Accounting for the fact I knew she was mad at me for hanging up on her yesterday, I didn't wake her to tell her I brought the teacup home for safe keeping. Waking her up would not work in my favor. Liz was an early riser which meant she went to bed early. Waking her up would've made her very grumpy and then I would've had to apologize, something I was not good at.

"It's missing," I said, entering the kitchen to the smell of burnt toast, my voice cracking, sounding like I hit puberty for the second time.

Liz sat at the small kitchen table she'd purchased at a secondhand store. She'd surfaced it with mosaic tiles to give it a shabby chic upcycling. Hearing my voice, she turned around, the teacup in her hand.

"What are you doing?!" I intoned like an accusation, pointing at her.

She glanced back at her sketchpad lying on the kitchen table. "Sketching and eating breakfast."

"That's the cup!"

Irritated, whipping out my phone, I showed her the picture I had taken of the Elizabeth Riley teacup after placing it back on the shelf. I don't know why I was agitated she was using the teacup. I was the one who brought it home. It was only a teacup, and she was only drinking tea. Maybe it was because she hadn't unpacked our stuff from the apartment yet. Sure, I could have done it, but work had been surprisingly busy for fall and when I got home, I had to check on the Riley House and get working on my 'honey do' list. Like I said, she worked from home, couldn't she unpack a little?

My wife glanced at the cup in her hands. "Sorry," she said, her apology sincere. "I wasn't feeling well so I made myself a cup of tea. I should've unpacked the mugs, but I didn't get around to doing it yet and I didn't want to boil water for my tea in a plastic cup."

I knew what was coming next, something about plastic giving off parabens, and parabens causing Alzheimer's. She had read an article on it, and it freaked her out, especially because her mother was in the first stages of dementia. She could drink out of plastic, but she would never reuse it or heat it.

"Use the cup," I said, feeling remorseful for my mania. "It has your name on it, it's meant to be."

Liz lifted the teacup above her head to read the bottom.

Meant to be . . . but did it have to be? Did I have to let this silly little teacup send me chasing a white rabbit? I guess it had to end this way. The same personality trait, call it drive, ambition, go-getter-ness, or monomania—this once believed positive attribute, now revealed as a major character flaw, had landed me my first date with Liz and helped me close my sales. It now coerced me to obsess over the teacup.

In hindsight, I realize I have a sensitivity. Not sensitive in the crying during a sappy movie kind of way, but sensitive to a world I couldn't see and frankly didn't believe existed until I entered Riley House. I was beginning to feel like the murderer gone mad in Edgar Allan Poe's short story, *The Tell-Tale Heart*. I checked off the obsessed box with an ease that was a tad startling. I wasn't quite hearing voices in Heaven and Hell, but I was definitely suffering from an acuteness of senses—a sensitivity, for a lack of a better word to describe the feeling that pervaded me every time I looked at the Elizabeth Riley teacup. I took solace in knowing ridding myself of the cup wouldn't land me in jail unless the teacup ended up being Queen Elizabeth II's, or the I's, and I destroyed a piece of history. But for now, I contented myself with knowing it didn't move by itself—my wife had taken it out of the dark, ugly china cabinet. All was well for now.

"Sorry," my wife said again, her free hand going for mine.

I instantly regretted my earlier tone. She didn't deserve this. I didn't deserve her. "It's okay," I said, taking a seat next to her. "I just didn't expect to see it missing from the cabinet.

It freaked me out a little.”

I hadn't told Liz I suspected the teacup was moved supernaturally, that my obsessive behavior surrounding the hand-painted teacup was to rule out the possibility that someone alive moved it. How could I explain to her how it made me feel when I couldn't even tell her that I was sorry? 'It freaked me out' was my half-baked attempt at an apology. That was all I could muster. Telling her, her very square, reliable husband now believed in ghosts was an impossibility.

I watched as my wife prepared another cup of tea. The cup suited her. I felt weird thinking it, but it did. It was fragile and small like her—beautiful. Liz pressed her teabag to the inside of the cup with a plastic spoon left over from last night's fast food dinner utensils, careful not to dip the spoon in the hot tea.

“An artist painted this before it went into the kiln,” she told me. “I wonder who Elizabeth Riley was, how she lived. I wonder if she made this teacup.”

I had wondered the same thing, not if Elizabeth Riley made the teacup, but who she was. I wanted to tell Liz I'd painted a portrait inside my head of who and what little Elizabeth looked like, but then I noticed the time. I had to get going. Instead of sharing my artsy side, I reached for a box of brown sugar Pop Tarts. It was the last sleeve. I offered her one. She declined with a shake of her head, adding honey to her tea.

I got to my feet, sliding the Pop Tart sleeve into my jacket pocket. I kissed the top of her head, a thing I did all the time. I liked doing it. Liz is significantly shorter than me and it emphasized her cuteness and her hair always smelled good—a mixture of tea tree oil and coconut. Kissing her head before I left for the morning had become second nature, the top of her head easily being her most kissed area. "Don't work too hard today, try to get some rest," I said, planting another kiss on the top of her head.

CHAPTER FOUR
Life is Full of Surprises

I got home from work early, stopping to perform my check at Riley House, which went without recourse thanks to the teacup being at my home–thank God. I felt silly for believing in ghosts. I concluded Riley House was a perfectly normal house as I walked the perimeter of the lower floor checking to make sure all the doors and windows were locked. It was no different from all the other homes on the market I had come by in my line of work. I had to chuckle at myself for jumping to conclusions, and even being scared. Scared of what? A teacup?

I also had a good laugh at my neurotic behavior. It was scary how one little wrinkle in my day could ruin the whole thing. I most likely have a compulsive disorder; my sister with the cat that can open doors always thought so.

After a peaceful check at my neighbor's house, I was happy to get home and happier yet when I opened the front door to the smell of a homecooked meal. It smelt amazing. The kind of smells that brought me back to my childhood—sautéed garlic and onions, fresh tomatoes and basil. My mother and grandmother had been terrific cooks, though now they preferred to dine out. I missed holiday gatherings centered around homecooked food made from scratch with recipes that had been in the Rossman family line for generations. It was left to Liz and me now to host our family gatherings—to which we have them catered. I didn't enjoy cooking, and as for Liz, well Liz, may be an expert at mixing paints in her studio to find the perfect shade but mixing ingredients in the kitchen was a different story. My wife's idea of cooking was eating dandelions out of the front yard. In the two years we were together, I think she cooked once, and after that I banned her from the kitchen on account of self-preservation.

They say life is full of surprises. I say that now with the wisdom of a man who should have known better than to trust life when you think it's throwing you a rainbow. But I was naive, sure I was surprised to see my wife cooking and even more surprised it smelled appetizing, especially since we thought our stove was in disrepair. But again, I thought it was just good fortune—Morris Benjamin Rossman: winner of the lottery. Could my day get any better?

Thinking back, I did have enough good sense to ask: "what's going on?"

I saw at once that the new gas range we had ordered had been delivered ahead of schedule—good fortune.

"I thought I'd cook tonight since we got the stove," my wife said, stirring homemade gravy with a wooden ladle. My wife's family is Italian. Gravy is red, tomato based, not brown or white and it takes a real chef to make it—something I didn't think Liz had in her.

She brought the ladle to my lips for me to try it. "My mother's recipe. Do you like it? I wanted to surprise you."

"I'm surprised," I confessed, noticing she unpacked the kitchen boxes from the old apartment and somehow made the disheveled kitchen look nice—homey. She cleaned the grime off the striped wallpaper and hung our wedding picture on the wall.

I kissed the top of her head. The smell of coconut acted as an aphrodisiac. "I'm glad you're feeling better. Tastes great and the kitchen looks great too."

Pleased, Liz went back to stirring the gravy on the stovetop. "I'm ahead of my commission; so, I figured I would give the house a little attention. You've been working so hard; it was time I got my hands dirty."

Again, the realization I didn't deserve Liz tickled my brain. Somehow, I got this terrific woman to be my wife.

I pulled her toward me, not caring if the ladle sunk into the pot. I kissed her deeply, the kind I normally reserved for after dinner, but what could I say, I really felt like the luckiest man in the world.

I hadn't noticed it right away, but as I brushed her dark hair off her shoulders, I realized my wife changed how she wore her hair. Liz loves headbands. She wore one every day, a way to keep her hair out of her face while she painted. Tonight, she had her hair subtly pinned back behind her ears. It was the kind of hairstyle girls in black and white mob movies sported. It suited her like the scalloped teacup, elegant and beautiful, and yet was somehow wrong.

CHAPTER FIVE
The Portrait

The weekend hit and I was happy to sleep in. I normally worked Saturdays, but after closing a huge sale, I took off. My game plan was to wake up naturally, then go for a long jog. The only good thing about moving out of the city were the trails in suburbia. Keyport, in particular, had nice trails; some ran by streams, others up hilly terrain. It was a long-distance runner's dream come true.

I did as I planned, waking up close to 9am to the smell of breakfast. My wife was always an early riser. One of those morning people who were as perky at 4am as normal people were at noon right before their lunch breaks. But since we got the new stove, she had been sneaking down extra early to make me breakfast. From scratch, I must add. She was really taking her newfound love of cooking to the next level. Yesterday it was quiche, today my favorite—muffins. I took a hard sniff in, trying to discern the variety of muffins Liz made—blueberry.

I hurriedly slipped on my running gear, which consisted of a long-sleeved Under Armour shirt and pants. I was just about to take the staircase when I noticed Liz's studio door was open. She always kept it closed. She didn't like anyone, including me, to see a painting before it was done. Defiantly, I popped my head in, curious to get a look at her latest commission.

On her easel was a sketch of her drinking out of the teacup. I entered, taking the necessary steps to stand in front of the easel. I must explain why this painting unnerved me as it did. Liz is a landscape artist. Trees, mountains, beaches, etcetera. In all the time I'd known her she never painted a portrait.

Liz painted with a mastery that always amazed me. Her paintings came to life as you looked at them. You could feel the crunching of leaves under your feet or the cold of the snow that iced the ground. She was the Bob Ross of landscape artists on steroids.

This self-portrait was no different, though it was just out of the sketch phase, outlined in pencil on canvas, only a few areas stroked with paint. The painting seemed alive, at least her eyes did. They looked impish. What startled me more than anything was those eyes. It wasn't that they housed a mischievous look hard to put into words, but the eyes in the painting were not my wife's. Liz had beautiful eyes, a blue gray she called slate, but the eyes in the portrait were green. At the time, I chalked it up to a thing I heard her mention called layering, applying coats of different colors to get a desired look.

"You like it?" Liz asked from behind me, her footfalls silent, her voice seemingly loud in her studio space.

I jumped, a prickling sensation traveled up my forearms. "Yeah, it's really good. It's just different from your happy trees and shrubs."

She locked her arm in mine as we stared at her portrait. My eyes were glued to the emerald eyes on the canvas, and to the way they floated above the bottom eyelid like a planet spinning out of orbit.

"I haven't done a portrait since art school, I'm a little rusty, but I thought it was time to shake off the rust."

CHAPTER SIX
Stranger Things

The next few weeks flew by and **Chrismukkah** was right around the corner. Chrismukkah is the joint celebration of Liz's Christmas with my Hanukkah. Liz's behavior continued to become increasingly strange. I could take her newfound love of cooking. I liked it. It was nice to eat a balanced meal. We were saving money, and my clothes were back to fitting properly.

I took it in stride when she turned in grunge rock for classical music. My father was an accomplished pianist, so to be honest, this little change in behavior was also welcomed. But nevertheless, it was strange. Liz always said her favorite instrument was the human voice—something she wasn't getting with Mozart, Bach, or Chopin.

The moment I knew something was really wrong was the day I went into her art room when she wasn't home. I was looking for tape to wrap her **Chrismukkah** presents while she was out shopping with one of her old friends. I think she said her name was Jackie, or was it Janice? I'm not sure, the important thing was she was out of the house. I opened the door and immediately took a step back, almost tripping over my feet. Hung up all over the walls of her studio were drawings of her sipping out of the Elizabeth Riley teacup.

I know this sounds crazy. I know it even as I recall it, but all of the portraits had green eyes and they all seemed to look at me, hundreds of beady jade stones staring in my direction. They all housed the same mischievous look the first portrait had. The sum of their stares together seemed to give off a palpable feeling, a tangible ominousness that caused me to take another step back.

I didn't like how the corner of my wife's lips in her many self-portraits curled up on one side. I hadn't noticed the expression when I saw the original sketch on her easel. It was as if she—I should say the woman in the portrait was mocking me, for the woman painted in life-like detail was not my wife. Somehow, by degree, I felt the woman in the portrait was influencing Liz. I know how it sounds—impossible, crazy, nutso, but I feel like since we moved into our new home she was becoming less and less of herself every day.

I had enough. I shut the door. Taking a moment to collect myself, I leaned against the closed studio door. No one could understand the horror in seeing the portraits. I can't accurately describe it. My legs felt like they were stuck in a block of cement, like time around me was slowing to a dreadful crawl and the only thing in real time was the glare of the portraits. They were so real, it seemed possible my wife's doppelgänger could step out of any of the portraits with that blasted teacup.

That was it—the teacup! I was losing focus. It was all

about the teacup. I realized my wife started acting strange around the same time I brought it home. Liz drank from it before she painted her first self-portrait, trading in rivers and trees for glaring eyes and curved smiles.

I had to get out of the house. I was really losing it and at that point I had this gut wrenching feeling I had already lost my wife. A tiny pit of nervous agitation spread through me like wildfire. I had to move, or I was going to succumb to the weight keeping me in place.

I dashed down the stairs, breaking free of my concrete shackles.

Something was wrong but what could I do? Who would believe me? My wife seemed happy, but at the same time seemed so much not like herself. She looked like her. Despite her new hairstyle rivaling Hollywood starlets from the 50's, she looked like herself—same slate eyes, dark hair, and bright smile, but what was going on behind her eyes and smile?

Maybe it was me. I was essentially working two jobs; I was a realtor by day and a handyman by night. Or maybe it was the teacup. It couldn't be me—no not me. That only left me with one thing to do. I had to destroy the teacup. I had to rid the house of it and get my wife back.

I'm sure most men would like all the ways my wife had changed, and I admit, at first, I liked them to. Who wouldn't want three home-cooked meals a day? I was not a fan of headbands or grunge rock and roll. But the more time that went by, I realized I didn't like all the ways Liz was changing, as subtle as some of the changes were. I felt like I was living a lie, like Liz wasn't my Liz anymore. Like every day that passed,

Liz lost a little more of the chutzpah that made me fall in love with her.

I barreled into the living room going for the china cabinet. The teacup wasn't there. I entered the kitchen. As if knowing what I planned to do, Liz came back early. She was sitting at the kitchen table sipping out of the teacup.

"Want a sip?" she asked, holding the teacup out for me to try. "It's a local blend."

I resisted smacking it out of her hand, afraid the hot tea would burn her. "No. No thank you."

I couldn't help but be startled by my wife as she sat there in our kitchen, her hair pulled back, her pink lips touching the scalloped border of the bone-china. It felt strange and wrong to feel anything for her that wasn't love. But every cell in my body was on alert—anticipating something—what, I didn't know.

"You're back early," I said, sliding my way to the front door.

"I just met Jackie for a quick bite to eat up the road. Then headed to Key Market for some more of this Keyport blend. You sure you don't want to try a cup?"

"Maybe later," I said, trying to sound natural, knowing Liz could see through my lack of acting skills. I reached for the doorknob. "I'm going to go for a jog. Be back in an hour or two."

With that, I grabbed my coat off the hook on the inside of the door and went outside. Luckily, I already had on my running outfit, as I was planning to run after I wrapped gifts. Sometimes I jogged to the park, sometimes I drove. It wasn't out of the ordinary that I got into my car.

I drove to the closest park, just letting the engine run as I thought. I didn't come up with much of an idea. The local police were worthless, and it wasn't like I could call the Ghostbusters to confirm a haunting or possession. I thought about going to a priest, but I'm Jewish, none of the Exorcist movies I watched had a rabbi in it.

Despondently staring out the window, I glimpsed the Keyport Historic Society through the leafless Sycamore trees lining the park's border. Last week, I had jogged past it noting it was only open on Saturdays. I was in luck; it was Saturday. I shut off the car engine and got out of my car, not sure exactly what I was looking for. But, I did hope to get a little more information about Riley House and Elizabeth Riley. From there I would make my next move, whether it be trying the cops again or going to my rabbi for advice.

I jogged across the street to the historical society mumbling profanities under my breath about my ex-neighbor Kevin. How did I forget about Kevin?! When I had brought the teacup home, I'd texted Kevin telling him I was going to keep it at my house until he got back into town. He hadn't responded. I hated it when people did that. A thumbs up emoji or a 'k' would have been a nice gesture on his part.

Before entering the Keyport Historical Society, I texted Kevin again letting him know I'd drop off his teacup, all he had to do was text me his new address. I made sure to add it wouldn't be an inconvenience as I was in the area. True, I had no idea where Kevin moved, and I didn't care. I would drive it to California if I had to.

I felt clever. I couldn't smash the teacup as I had originally planned, my wife was too attached. But it was Kevin's, and if he wanted it back, he had every right to it. My wife would have to accept this. Disaster would be averted on both sides. My mood lightened. This seemed like a better course of action than involving the police or seeking religious guidance.

While I waited for Kevin to get back to me, I went into the octagon shaped building of the Keyport Historical Society. It had to be one of the strangest buildings I had ever seen. It was one big three-dimensional stop sign, in shape only—it was painted white.

I was greeted by two jovial, large women that could have been sisters. They had the same almond shaped eyes and white curly hair that always reminded me of show poodles. I got the distinct impression they didn't get a lot of visitors despite the Keyport Historical Society only being open on Saturdays.

"How can we help you?" the larger of the two women asked.

"Do you know anything about Riley House?"

The woman's eyes lit up. "You must be Morris Rossman."

I was taken aback. How did this woman know my name?

It was as if she read my mind.

"Randall told us a young man by the name of Morris Rossman was house sitting for Riley House in Kevin's stead."

"Oh, yeah, that's me," I said, extending my hand, relaxing when I realized Randall was Officer Randall. Boy was this a small town. "Call me Morey."

They both shook my hand eagerly. The second woman, Sarah, added, "Randall didn't say you were young and handsome." To that, I blushed. She went on to say, "Kevin always cared about that house. Said no place felt like home but Riley House. Always said he didn't think he could leave it. I'm glad he did."

I smiled, knowing it was an awkward smile that looked like faeries were poking me with pins. Kevin was not exactly on my holiday card list.

Sarah shook my hand again, reintroducing herself as Kevin's niece.

More good fortune.

"Do you know Kevin's new address?"

"I do." Sarah pulled a sticky pad from a small desk against the far wall and scribbled down the address for me. In the meantime, the first woman who had greeted me, Camilla, went to a tall, wooden file cabinet.

Sarah handed me the address on a hot pink sticky note. I folded it and put it in my coat pocket, zippering it shut, eternally grateful.

Camilla was busy at the copy machine. These women were efficient. We could use them at the office.

A few moments later Camilla walked over to Sarah and me, handing me a stack of photocopied articles. I scanned them as she talked.

"The Riley House is somewhat of a celebrity in Keyport."

I looked up at that. It was weird to hear someone

address Riley House like it was a person.

"She's a beautiful building designed by Keyport's very own Charles Riley, but most of her life she's been abandoned."

"Why's that?" I asked. There was something in the way Camilla talked about the house, how her eyes seemed to swell with sadness at it being abandoned.

Sarah answered. "Because of the murder of course."

"Murder?!" I sounded like a parrot. My wife was from Keyport, and the only thing she'd ever said about Riley House was that it was built by a famous architect. I would have remembered if she'd told me about a murder. Neither Liz nor Kevin said anything about that.

I wondered if the realtor of Riley House was telling families about the murder. Legally, it was their obligation. It did explain why a beautiful house in better condition than the one Liz and I bought was still on the market.

"It was a big scandal," Sarah added.

"If you have the time, I'd love to hear the story from a local."

Camilla seemed thrilled; her smile told me she was going to tell me the real story. "As you can imagine the Riley's were very wealthy."

"Millionaire's Corner," I chirped.

Camilla seemed pleased I knew the basics, graciously nodding at me with a warm smile that reminded me of Betty White. "Elizabeth, lady of Riley House, was a lovely, young woman who married Benjamin Riley. Benjamin was the grandson of Charles Riley and was just as lovely as she was. Though Elizabeth had humble roots, Benjamin came from old money and made his fortune the way his father before him made his—foreign trade. They were the envy of the town. They seemed like a happy couple but there were rumors."

I couldn't help myself, I leaned in. "Rumors?"

"Rumors that Elizabeth Riley was having an affair."

It was hard for me to imagine the little girl I envisioned sipping out of the delicate teacup as a woman and adulteress. I had gotten it all wrong.

Camilla pulled over a seat from the desk next to the copy machine and sat, rubbing her knees as she spoke. "I know having an affair is not big news these days, but in Elizabeth's and Benjamin's day it was. I was a child then and I remember my mother and grandmother whispering about it. You see, back then men cheated on their wives, but wives never cheated on their husbands."

"Then poor Benjamin Riley was found dead, and Elizabeth disappeared," Sarah added.

"How did he die? What do you mean disappeared?" I knew I should have just headed for Kevin's—my end goal was to get rid of the teacup—but I was curious, too curious.

Camilla and Sarah tried to beat each other to the punch line. "Poisoned," they said together, their eyes alive with gossip.

"He was poisoned to death," Camillia said, reaching for the stack of articles she had handed me.

She pointed to the article on the top of the stack. "At first, everyone thought Benjamin Riley died of natural causes. It looked like a heart attack, though he wasn't much older than you are now. You see, weak hearts ran in the Riley family. Most of the men died young, so no one thought much about it. But when Elizabeth was nowhere to be found, a fancy doctor from the city did an autopsy and traces of arsenic showed up in his stomach."

"Rat poison," I said.

"They think he drank it with his morning tea," Sarah informed me solemnly, bowing her head in respect for the late Benjamin Riley.

"Tea," I mumbled to myself, my stomach tightening into a knot that almost doubled me over.

"That's what the post reported. It's in one of the articles," Camilla said. "He was found dead, tea stains all over his dress shirt and vest."

"Who poisoned Benjamin? Was it Elizabeth?" I asked. I couldn't shake the image of Benjamin Riley sipping from the rose painted teacup, his lips pressed against the scalloped rim before collapsing dead—poisoned.

"No one knows for sure. It's still an open case as far as I know," Sarah said. "Do you know if it's still open?" she asked, looking to her counterpart.

"Still an open case, colder than any cold case Keyport ever had," Camilla confirmed.

So much for Keyport's low crime rate.

Sarah went on, "Most Keyporters think it was Elizabeth Riley. She had a motive. Benjamin Riley was not the kind of man that would have granted her a divorce. He was a politician and a thing like a divorce would've ruined his political career. The strangest thing about it was Elizabeth never showed up again and never withdrew any money from their bank accounts. It's like the day Benjamin died, she vanished into thin air."

CHAPTER SEVEN

Jacklyn Riley

I thanked Camilla and Sarah for their time and help and eagerly made my way back to my car and got in. I folded the copied articles in a perfect square and slid them into my coat pocket opposite the pocket with the sticky note denoting Kevin's address. I checked my phone—nothing from Kevin. Annoyed, I tossed it on the passenger's seat. Unzipping my other pocket, I pulled out the sticky note with his address on it. I wanted to know how long it was going to take to get to Kevin's. I was hoping he didn't actually move to the Golden State.

I stared at the address dumbfounded. I recognized it. Well, not completely, but I recognized the street. He lived on Cherry Blossom. Main Street forked through town turning into Cherry Blossom. It was the path I usually jogged.

My face flushed with anger. I was annoyed Kevin still lived in town and had me checking on Riley House. It would have been only a short drive back and forth for him. Keyport wasn't that big. The way he'd been talking, I thought he moved hours away.

I decided to take the long way home and drove down

Cherry Blossom. I had just made it onto Cherry Blossom when I saw Kevin standing in front of the entrance for Keyport Cemetery. My foot hit the brake with a screech. I pulled off to the shoulder of the road, throwing my car into park. Hopping out of my car, I franticly looked for him, turning my head right to left and then back again with a rapidity that nearly gave me whiplash. It had only taken a moment to unbuckle and get out of my car, where could he have gone off to?

I entered the cemetery, assuming he had to have entered. It was cold there. The cemetery was situated on a large hill that butted up against the Hudson River and I could feel the chill coming off the water. The cemetery was a mixture of small headstones, most of them so old you couldn't read the names anymore. Time's unforgiving hand left only shallow traces of letters and dates. There was no sign of a grounds keeper. Even in December, it was obvious the grass hadn't been cut in a long time. The tall grass, turned to brown husks by the winter, whipped back and forth against the aged stones in the breeze. This produced a sound like the dull muttering of voices, nothing distinct, just an unearthly moan that made me feel uncomfortable; as if the moans were not the result of the beating of grass blades on stone, but the voices of the fallen who I treaded on in my pursuit to find Kevin.

I was used to Jewish cemeteries where headstones were in lines alphabetized by last name. Keyport Cemetery seemed haphazard, like people were buried in any little space that still had room, headstones jutting out in all different directions. I got the sinking feeling that once you entered Keyport you never left—that I too was going to end up under one of those jutting tombstones without a name. Part of me wanted to get in my car, drive home, grab Liz and head back to New York City. But the other part of me, the damnable part of me, had to see this through to the end.

Shoving my hands in my pockets, I quickened my pace, jogging down snaking paths in search of Kevin. I eventually found him standing in front of a headstone. "Why didn't you text me back?!" I barked, sounding nastier than I meant to.

Kevin looked happy to see me, a smile peeking out from his beard and moustache. "How's it going neighbor?"

"I've been better." Dropping all platitudes. "I want to drop off your teacup. Are you going to be here for a while? I'll head home, grab it and head right back."

He glanced over me curiously, "Teacup?"

I gestured with my hands, cupping them together and bringing them to my lips as if to explain it to a caveman. "The small one with roses painted on it. It was in the hutch in the living room. You know, Elizabeth Riley's teacup."

He scratched the side of his head. "Well, it's not mine then, is it? It's Elizabeth's."

I tried to control my temper, my hands balling into fists at my sides. "It was in your house, so it makes it your teacup. Wait right here—I'll be right back."

"Afraid I can't wait," Kevin said.

I was at my breaking point. Holding back tears and wrecking balls. "Why's that?!"

"I have to get back. My boy's waiting on me."

"Give me fifteen minutes. Twenty tops. Please Kevin." I reached for my cell phone. "Give me your number again. I must've put it in my phone wrong." I patted down my pockets. "Crap, one moment, I left it in my car."

I jogged to my car not giving him a moment to say no. I grabbed my phone off the passenger's seat and jogged back. Kevin was nowhere to be seen. I felt like screaming. In fact, I did. "Kevin!" I shouted over and over again, tears of frustration stinging the back of my throat. My eyes landed on the tombstone Kevin had been standing in front of. It was Benjamin Riley's grave.

I read the tombstone out loud, my voice carried on the wind sounding like an echo. "Benjamin Kevin Riley." The year of his birth and death were engraved, but Elizabeth Rose Riley's date of death was never added to the headstone. It was true—no one ever did find out what happened to her.

There was something else written on the headstone. I couldn't quite read it. It was partially obstructed by a scrubby looking boxwood. I knelt to move the branches out of the way. It was another name: Jacklyn Ann Riley.

Neither Camilla nor Sarah from the Keyport Historical Society mentioned Benjamin and Elizabeth having a child. I reasoned if I had taken the time to read the articles Camilla gave me, I would've found Jacklyn's name amongst them.

I pulled out my phone and typed in the name. Jacklyn Ann Riley popped up all over Google. She was a wealthy philanthropist living in the neighboring shore town. It would take me thirty minutes to get there.

It's amazing what you can find on the internet. Interestingly enough, nothing popped up about the murder of Jacklyn Riley's father or the disappearance of her mother.

Maybe Keyport hushed it up or more likely the old newspaper articles hadn't been scanned to the internet yet.

I'm not entirely sure what led me to drive to Jacklyn Riley's shore house. Curiosity more than anything I suppose. It was too early to head back to the house. I wanted to walk in and act like everything was normal, that I just went on my usual jog and ran into Kevin.

I had already decided that I was going to tell my wife I ran into him and that he asked me to drop the teacup off. But what I was actually going to do was drive it to Keyport Cemetery and throw it in the river. Liz would never know the difference and Kevin didn't want it back. It would be for the best. But for this to work, I had to get the timing right. If I went back to the house now it would make Liz suspicious, especially after I left the house abruptly this morning. I didn't want to give Liz any reason not to trust what I said. I feared if she doubted my motives, she would want to come for the ride to drop the teacup off. That would unnecessarily complicate things.

With that settled, I walked up the granite steps of a beautiful beach mansion. It was a historical property, there was no doubt about that. It had large Corinth columns that rose three stories. With four large, ocular dormers, it made quite the impression. It was a corner property which raised the value. I placed the house's market worth at an easy 3.5 million.

I rang the doorbell, suddenly aware of my appearance. I was in my Under Armour and a black winter coat. If I had a ski mask, I'd look like a ninja. Or, knocking on a house like this, a burglar—oh well, it was too late to turn back now.

The door opened and I was greeted by a maid. I knew

this because she had a bucket of cleaning supplies in her hands. No heiress would clean their own toilets.

"Hello, is Jacklyn home?"

"Mrs. Jackie is in the study," the lady told me in a thick accent I couldn't quite place. "Is she expecting you?"

"Who is it Esmeralda?" a voice called from down the hall.

"Morris Rossman," I said, loud enough for Jacklyn to hear me.

"It's a Mr. Morris Rossman ma'am."

A woman with long dark hair emerged from behind a carved mahogany door wearing an outfit similar to mine, minus the winter coat. She was a runner, her body screamed gym rat. If I'm being honest, she had a better figure than Liz. Jacklyn Riley had all the right curves in all the right places.

I quickly introduced myself, putting my hand out for her to shake it. "Morris Rossman. I've been looking after Riley House." I took out my wallet and handed her my business card.

She glanced over it approvingly as if the business card proved I was neither ninja nor burglar.

I had expected Jacklyn Riley to be old, really old, like Camilla and Sarah from the Keyport Historical Society; however, Jacklyn didn't appear to be—not at first glance anyway. Her hands gave her away. She'd had work done, that much was obvious: face lift, eye lift, who knows what else, but her hands were covered in old age spots and wrinkles. I wondered why plastic surgeons hadn't found a way to reverse the signs of aging in hands yet.

After courteously returning the handshake, Jacklyn smiled at me with a smile that was meant for television and invited me in. "I'm afraid I can't talk long Mr. Rossman. I was just about to head out for a jog on the boardwalk."

This panicked me. I didn't know what I wanted from Jacklyn Riley, but I didn't want our time cut short.

"Please, call me Morey. I don't want to hold you up. Perhaps we could talk while we jogged. That is, if you don't mind the company."

She hesitated for a moment thinking it over.

"I promise I'm not a killer," I said, thinking that sounded like something a killer would say.

She laughed. "The boards are a public space, so it wouldn't be the best place to commit a murder. And besides," she said, tapping on my business card that she placed on the console table near the front door, "Esmeralda and I have your name and number."

Seeming to like the idea of sticking to her schedule and regarding me as harmless, she gestured toward the door I just came through. I was gracious for her time. I'm sure heiress philanthropists were busy people.

We jogged down the block to the boardwalk. It was warmer on the boards than it had been in Keyport Cemetery. You could hear the waves hitting the beach. It was the perfect temperature and location for a long-distance jog.

"Riley House . . . I haven't heard that name in a long time," Jacklyn confessed as we started down the planks.

"Did you ever live there?" I asked, keeping pace with her, which was difficult. I was significantly taller than her, by a good foot from what I could tell.

"Until my father died."

"Father? So, Benjamin Riley was your father?" My assumption that Jacklyn's name was on the family headstone owing to the fact she was the child of Benjamin and Elizabeth was correct.

"I was adopted, but yes, Benjamin Riley was my father."

"Do you mind if I ask what happened?" I was hoping Jacklyn wasn't getting turned off by my assertiveness. I was sure she answered questions like this all the time, but probably not from strangers who knocked on her door, regardless of a business card that would have had Patrick Bateman from *American Psycho* jealous.

"We thought it was a heart attack. He was a high stress man. So stressed he caused his hair to prematurely gray. We believed his heart just gave out, but an autopsy turned up rat poison in his system."

She sounded like the article Camilla quoted. I imagined she must have been very young when it happened and knew only what others told her.

Jacklyn added, after a long pause, "It could have been an accident, the house always had rats. I hope it was at least."

"Yeah, my house is loaded with them. I guess it comes with the territory of living so close to the river. I've been trying to talk my wife into getting a cat." I hadn't mentioned to Jacklyn I lived across the street from Riley House and thought I should mention it now. "My wife and I bought the house across the street, that's how I ended up taking care of Riley House in the first place."

She smiled, a flash of a Hollywood smile. "Billandbeth. That's a lovely home."

I fell back a few paces. "What?"

"You didn't know your house has a name?"

"No," I said really confounded. I was a realtor after all, and I had done a lot of research on the house before we bought it. I wondered if Liz knew about the house's name, her being a local and all.

"Your house was named after my stepmother."

"Elizabeth Riley? I asked, my brain foggy as I jogged to catch up with her.

"Yes Elizabeth Riley," she said with a slight chuckle that made me feel a tad stupid. "It's the name the Keyporters gave your house. My stepmother was having an affair with William Blair, the owner of the house you now live in. He was married to an Elizabeth. But my stepmother went by Beth, so it was a little inside joke amongst the ne'er-do-wells."

"Keyport has a mean streak," I said.

"Little towns like Keyport thrive on gossip, always have and always will."

"Was it true? Was Elizabeth—Beth—cheating on Benjamin?"

"I can't say. I was too young."

"And your stepmother, you never heard from her after your father died?"

Jacklyn jogged in a 'u' shape heading back in the direction we came. I followed. "No never. Her suitcase was missing along with most of her clothes from her closet. It was a hard time for me. My stepmother had always been very loving. She'd throw the most wonderful tea parties. It was hard to believe she could do something like that and abandon me."

I couldn't resist. "Speaking of tea, I found a teacup at the house." I pulled out my phone, showing her the picture I'd taken as evidence to prove I put it back in the hutch. I did my best to keep my phone steady, not an easy task while jogging.

Jacklyn took my phone from me to get a better look. "I can't believe after all these years it survived."

"You recognize it?"

She handed me back my phone. "It was my stepmother's favorite teacup. She had it since she was a little girl and drank her morning, noon, and evening tea from it. She used to have the whole set, but that was the only piece that had survived her childhood. She cherished it."

"Geez, you think if she cherished it, she would've taken it with her when she skipped town."

Jacklyn seemed to think on this, her eyebrows trying to furrow despite the Botox. "You're right, you would think so. I guess it was her way of leaving it to me."

"But you never took it with you when you left?" I asked, wondering how close the two actually were. I noticed she referred to Benjamin as her father and Elizabeth as her stepmother.

"No, I never did," she admitted, her eyes glassy. Seeing it made me think of her and what she did to me. Made me feel all this anger . . . I just had to try to move on."

I felt bad for judging Jacklyn's relationship with Elizabeth so quickly. I didn't blame her for thinking of her in terms of a 'stepmother' rather than a mother. After all,

Elizabeth Riley had packed her bags and skipped town leaving her daughter, adopted or not, behind. There was no getting around the fact Elizabeth Riley abandoned Jacklyn. Being adopted myself, I sympathized. I'd be devastated if the woman I came to know and love as mother abandoned me after my biological parents did. The betrayal would cut even deeper, carving out a wound that would never heal.

I didn't want to come off insensitive; but, here was another chance to get rid of the teacup. Like I said, I worried Liz may want to go for the ride to drop it off at Kevin's. She could easily accompany me to Jacklyn's and all would be right with the world.

"Do you want the teacup back? I could drop it off to you if you'd like."

We jogged off the boards back down her block. "Can you give me some time to think about it?"

Oh, crap what did I do?! I couldn't toss it now, not when I offered it to her. I chuckled nervously. "How much time?" Her eyes darted to me, clearly my response was atypical. I knew that, but I was desperate to get the thing out of my home. "I'm sorry," I said, putting my acting skills to the test yet again. "It's just . . . well, it's just that we're trying to clear the clutter."

"I understand. Can I let you know by tonight?"

"That's perfect," I said, stopping by my car. Jacklyn leaned against it, catching her breath. This jog was more of a warmup for me, however Jacklyn seemed winded. I took the pause to ask, "Did you ever notice anything strange about Riley House?" I didn't want to come straight out and say I thought the teacup was haunted or something. I wanted Jacklyn to take it, but I figured if anyone knew about the strangeness it would be the woman who grew up in the house with the teacup and the very woman who owned it. She herself said Elizabeth—Beth—drank from it morning, noon and night.

Jacklyn turned slightly away from me. This piqued my interest. I moved closer.

"People say they've seen Benjamin."

"Have you?" I asked, nudging even closer.

"Once. Only once. He was in the living room near the hutch that held my stepmother's teacup. I thought at the time it was his way of telling me what Elizabeth had done to him. Not long after that, I came to live with my grandmother here," she said, looking up at her sprawling beach mansion, "and have been here ever since."

I was distraught. If she believed Elizabeth murdered her father, she wouldn't want the teacup, but so as not to look bad by declining my offer outright, she asked for time to think it over. That meant one more night with it at my house, with my wife, before I could toss it in the Hudson.

Riley House having a known ghost was news to me, but then again so was Benjamin Riley's murder. I was really going to let Kevin have it the next time I saw him. But to be fair, I wouldn't have believed him. I didn't believe in those types of things until I moved to Keyport. Before the move, I never would have entertained the idea, but now it was the only thing that made sense. The doors and windows were locked by my very own experienced hands and I had the only key. The ghost of Benjamin Kevin Riley moving around a teacup that belonged to his wife as his only means to signal it was she who murdered him seemed like the most obvious thing in the world. Either way, the teacup had bad aura, juju, feng shui, or whatever you wanted to call it and had to go. I reasoned, it deserved it. As if a teacup, an inanimate object, deserved anything but it was, according to Jacklyn, a prized possession of a murderess and had no place in my home or as far as I was concerned in all of Keyport, New York.

Jacklyn teared up, stirring me from my convictions. "Not a day goes by that I don't think of my father. We had a special bond."

I'm a big softy when it comes to people crying, especially when they do it because of me. I brought this about, me visiting her, dredging up old memories. I hugged her. "I'm sorry. I shouldn't have pried."

I truly felt that way. It did neither of us any good, as I was pretty confident she wasn't going to take the teacup, and her tears showed no signs of stopping.

"Why couldn't she leave us be?"

I was way out of my element. Liz was not a crier, a thing I normally was grateful for, but that meant I didn't have much practice in comforting. I went ahead and gave it the ole' college try, using what I learned from Camilla and Sarah about the late Benjamin Riley. "Maybe she was afraid Benjamin would come after her. It sounds like he had the power and money to do it. Not that that was an excuse," I added quickly, because it wasn't.

She wiped a tear. "I often think about how different my life would have turned out if he'd just let her go."

I squeezed her, not sure what else to do. She lifted

herself on her toes, pressing her lips to mine. In surprise, my lips parted. She deepened the kiss. I separated us gently by pushing on her shoulders. "I'm sorry Jacklyn, I'm married." She ran her hand up my thigh and went in for another kiss. To my shame, I let her kiss me. Jacklyn was probably old enough to be my grandmother, but she looked like a dark-haired Dolly Parton, and then there were her tears. If kissing me comforted her, then I should let it happen. After all, it was my curiosity that caused the rainstorm. I felt confused, like my head was underwater and not enough oxygen was getting to my brain. Not in the intoxicating way love makes one feel but the suffocation that comes with the fear of losing it. I was confused about Liz, worried about her. My anxieties about my wife ran into an endless well of worries now joined by Jacklyn's tears and kisses.

Coming to my senses, I stepped back. "Jacklyn, I should go. I'm sorry. Call me if you want me to drop off the teacup." I whipped out another business card from my wallet, forgetting in my blunder I had handed her one earlier. I fumbled for my keys. Finding them, I opened the driver side door and got in. Jacklyn stood on the sidewalk crying.

"Crap," I mumbled. I couldn't leave her like that. I climbed out of my car. Taking her hand, "Jacklyn, I'm so sorry for stopping by like this. I am. You're terrific. If I wasn't married, well, I wouldn't be driving home right now. But I am, so I have to go. I hope we can be friends." She nodded. I hugged her again, her tears drying up. This time she kept her lips to herself.

Satisfied I did what I could to remedy the situation, I

got back in my car. With a wave goodbye, I was on my way home.

CHAPTER EIGHT

The Rats

I got home later than I meant to. My wife already had my lunch waiting for me. A homemade potpie sat on one of the fancy white dishes we received from my grandmother as a wedding gift. Liz sat at the table, her potpie untouched. Elizabeth Riley's favorite teacup steamed with tea, most likely that Keyport blend she'd been raving about.

"I tried calling you," Liz said, the moment I stepped over the threshold.

"Sorry. I ended up stopping at the historical society looking for info on our house. I was trying to find some pictures of it in its glory days. I want to make sure our reno is a good one," I rambled off in a lie. The guilt of Jacklyn's kiss and the just told lie used to cover it up made me sick. I was not a liar; it fell into line with not being a good actor.

There was nothing I could do now about the two kisses, for that was all there was. But I could make good on visiting Keyport Historical Society in the pursuit of information on Billandbeth and planned to do just that the following Saturday.

Liz's face brightened up. "That's a great idea! You find

anything?”

Guilt swarmed inside me. I could still taste Jacklyn Riley. Her particular flavor was a cross between peppermint and cherry ChapStick. In a panic, I realized the lingering scent of her perfume clung to my coat. “Not yet, but I’m sure I will.”

Another lie. My stomach did a back flip.

Liz approached me, her anger melted away by my conjured deception. Normally, I would’ve kissed the top of her head hello, but I didn’t want to risk Liz smelling Jacklyn’s perfume. I know I didn’t do anything, but that was part of the problem. I let it all happen. I yanked the front door back open.

“Where are you going? You’re not hungry? You’re always hungry after a run . . .”

“I think I’m coming down with something, my stomach’s bothering me.” That was the first truthful thing I said to Liz all day and it made me feel a little better saying it even if it were under false pretenses. “I’m going to do my check at Riley House then go lie down. You go ahead and eat lunch without me.”

Relief—I was outside, halfway to Riley House. I pulled my coat to my nose. I’d made the right choice in getting out of there. There was no way Liz wouldn’t have smelled the perfume. I felt stupid for not leaving my coat in the car when I went inside. I would not make that mistake again. I would leave my coat in the car and head straight to the shower as soon as I made sure Riley House was locked up.

I did my walk-through on autopilot. I’d walked the lower level of Riley House so often I knew it like the back of my hand. As what had become a ritual, I stopped in the living room before leaving.

I stared at the empty hutch, my stomach performing a double somersault that could have landed it on the Olympic team if only organs could try out. The teacup was still at my house, but just thinking about it sent a wave of nausea through me.

My phone dinged. It was a text message from Jacklyn.

'Hi Morey. It's Jacklyn Riley. I just wanted to say sorry for my behavior and thank you for listening to me today.'

I groaned outwardly. There was nothing in her message about the teacup. I wondered if I should text her about it, or if that would come off too pushy, but I needed to make sure she didn't want it before it joined the other trash in the Hudson River. I cursed myself for complicating matters. It may have been Benjamin Riley who moved the teacup, but that didn't explain what was happening to Liz. The only logical explanation, if I could call it that, was that the teacup was somehow poisoning her. Just thinking that caused my pulse to race. I wanted my Liz as far away from murder and poison as humanly possible. It killed me to think of her sipping tea out of Elizabeth Riley's teacup while I waited on Jacklyn's response.

I decided to go for it. I spoke out loud to myself, over pronouncing the syllables as I drafted my message with the text to speech feature. "No-prob-lem. Did-you-want-me-to-drop-off-E-liz-a-beth's—"

No sooner had her name escaped my lips, then a thud from under my feet sounded. It caused me to jump, sending my phone skittering across the floor. My heart beat against my chest like I'd just finished a sprint. Focusing on the quiet, I waited to see if the sound would come again.

The idea that thud could be the ghost of Benjamin Riley sent a shiver up my back like my spine was a xylophone hitting shrilling notes. I eyed my phone from across the room, but I dared not move to retrieve it. In all the time I had been checking on Riley House, never had I heard a noise like that. It was as if someone was walking upside down on the floorboards under me. I thought of the rats and the rat poison that did poor Benjamin Riley in. The noise could've been rats and/or all sorts of creepy crawlers in the basement, though I hadn't seen any evidence of droppings in the house. Or, I reasoned as my pulse surged, it very well could be the ghost of Benjamin Riley. Maybe he knew I planned on tossing Elizabeth's teacup in the river. But if so, why would that elicit a response from him. He should be thanking me. She'd poisoned him.

Or had she? In the still of the house, I thought again about Elizabeth Riley packing up her belongings and leaving her 'cherished' teacup behind. Something about that seemed off—really off. And my wife's strange behavior didn't seem like she was possessed by a man but by a woman. So that ruled out anything funny going on with the ghost of Benjamin Riley and my wife. That led me to believe there had to be two ghosts, the other one being Elizabeth Riley. It made sense, it was her teacup—her cherished teacup.

I went for full blown crazy, or maybe it was the only sane thing left to do. "Elizabeth Riley is that you?" I asked in a whisper, a cool sweat dripping down my temple. It was silly to fear ghosts, it's the living that can hurt you, not them. But I was scared.

More silence, a silence that was too quiet, like I stepped into the void I so often felt I was in while at Riley House.

Things weren't adding up for me. Benjamin Riley was poisoned. He was dead; I saw his grave, but no one knew what happened to Elizabeth Riley. Why would her ghost be here in Riley House when she went off to start a new life away from it?

I realized I knew very little about Elizabeth Riley, besides her love of tea.

I pulled the articles Camilla copied for me at the historical society from my coat pocket, unfolding them as quietly as I could. I hadn't had the chance to read them yet, but now I found myself overcome with a burning desire to. I scanned the articles, coming across a picture of Elizabeth Riley. She was beautiful. You could tell even in the blurry newspaper. She had light hair and light eyes, that could have been blue or green. I felt unsettled, noticing her blonde hair was pinned back in the fashion Liz had adopted.

It was hard to keep my hands steady, but I managed to flip through the papers looking for more pictures. I was too shaken to read after seeing the first photograph of Elizabeth Riley. I came across Benjamin's and Elizabeth's wedding picture. Elizabeth's hair was pinned back in the same way as the first photograph. She wore a modest dress and a long veil that trailed behind her on the ground. Benjamin—well Benjamin oddly looked a lot like me. He had the same chin and hair line that went off to the side. From the picture, I could tell he, like myself, had the striking combination of very dark hair and very light eyes. A combo my sister was always jealous of.

"Elizabeth Riley . . . Beth what happened to you?" I asked as I stared at the picture of her in her wedding gown. The same thud sounded. I froze, hearing a scurry. Most likely it was a rat. Our basement was infested with them, I knew the sound. Liz had said rats had always been a big problem in Keyport thanks to the river. I had set traps in the basement—the humane kind to keep Liz happy. They hadn't worked. I had wanted to go with the old-fashioned rat poison. The same kind that may have accidentally poisoned Benjamin Riley or deliberately murdered him, but it wasn't worth getting Liz upset. I was just going to bring home a kitten one day and let it loose in the basement.

As I stood there listening and thinking about rats and mice, and God knows what other kind of vermin in the basement, I came to realize a peculiarity of Riley House. It did not have a door leading to the basement. Riley House and Billandbeth were built by the same builder, the famous architect Charles Riley. I had noticed a lot of similarities between my house and Riley House, with Riley House just being on a grander scale. I thought about our basement. It was a half basement: half crawl space, half walk down. In all the time I walked Riley House, I never noticed an entrance into the basement. We had two. We had a door off the entry leading into the basement from the inside of the house and from the outside we had a Bilco door, the kind made famous in movies where everyone ran to the cellar during a tornado.

Riley House, a mansion, not having a door to the

basement by way of inside the house or outside just seemed crazy, particularly for a master architect's country home. I'd supposed it could have been a flaw in the design, something Charles Riley corrected in future projects, or I could have just missed it.

Like I said, I knew the inside of the house like the back of my hands, so after picking up my phone, I went outside looking for the entry point into the basement. After walking the perimeter of the house several times, I determined there was no walk down into the basement from inside or outside the house, but there were small windows in the sandstone foundation, that could be opened. I knelt shining my phone flashlight under the house.

From as far as I could tell the basement was just a crawl space. That would explain why there was not a door to the basement. It would've been a door to nowhere. The crawl space had a floor of dirt and was shallow. It would be hard for a grown man to fit comfortably. But I was tall and lean and certain that I could squeeze into the crawl space.

I had this horrible idea that excited me. I called my wife and said I was running to Walmart for Nyquil and Tums and asked her if she needed anything. I headed to Home Depot instead and bought gloves, a small hand shovel, a compact floodlight, and a Snickers bar to tide me over.

Getting back to Riley House, I took off my winter coat and got down on my stomach. With the hand shovel in one hand and the floodlight in the other, I pulled myself into the crawl space with my elbows. I slowly made my way to the spot below the living room. Once I was under the location I believed to be in front of the hutch, the spot I had first noticed the teacup, I started to dig.

What felt like hours later, cramps running up and down my arms and neck, I struck something. I hastily cleared away the dirt with my blistered palms. Digging with the gloves on had become too cumbersome, they didn't fit right. I ditched them early on in my endeavor for efficiency. Through the loose soil, I could make out what appeared to be bones. Adrenaline fueling me, I frantically scratched at the dirt with my nails. I did so as if the person trapped in the crawl space was still alive and if I could just get to them in time, I could save them. I felt this need, this compelling desire to help whoever was buried in this unmarked grave. My fingernails broke off against a rib cage. I followed it up digging for the skull, locks of light blonde matted hair shone in the floodlight. It was Elizabeth Riley.

CHAPTER NINE
The Confession

While I waited for Officer Randall to get to Riley House, I decided to call Jacklyn. I sat down on the front steps of the mansion and dialed her. It went to voicemail. 'You reached Jackie R's voicemail leave a message and I'll get back to you.' I was in the process of leaving a message when she called me back.

"Benjamin," she said into the phone groggy.

"No, it's Morris Rossman. I stopped by today. I'm sorry to have woken you."

"Oh, hi Morey. It's okay, I dozed off on the couch reading a book. How are you?"

"I'm fine, but I do have some news. I guess I thought I should be the one to tell you."

"Tell me what?" She asked, sounding more alert.

"I think I found your stepmother."

Silence.

I saw how that statement was confounding, I went to explain. "I dug up the crawl space at Riley House and found human remains. The Keyport police are on their way now."

Trying to sound like the cops from TV, "I don't know how long it will take to confirm the DNA evidence, but I believe the body buried in the crawl space is that of Elizabeth Riley."

Sobs sounded over the phone. I guess I messed that up big time. I should've told her in person or passed it off to Officer Randall. I was a realtor not a cop. I was beyond out of my element; I might as well have been from a different planet.

"Don't cry. We don't know it's her, not for sure, but I was hoping after how upset you were today, this could give you some closure. Your stepmother didn't abandon you."

"Thank you Benjamin," she finally got out.

I didn't correct her. She was clearly overburdened with grief and confused.

* * *

"Let me get this straight," Officer Randall said, using the step I was sitting on as a platform to tie his shoe, his notepad firmly tucked under his chin. A few officers emerged from their vehicles with flashlights and shovels. Officer Randall, once finished with his laces, stood tall returning his notepad to his hand, pulling out the pen that was tucked behind his right ear. "You just decided to dig up the crawl space?"

"Not exactly." My adrenaline rush had passed leaving me exhausted and cold. I was crashing. We had been through this twice now, but I wanted to go home so I attempted an abridged version of the day's events again. "I went to the historical society and talked to Camilla and Sarah, then I ran into Kevin at the cemetery, then I met Jacklyn Riley."

"And they said you should dig up the crawl space?"

Why couldn't he just listen. "No, they didn't. I heard a

noise, and I investigated it."

"And you think the bones belong to Elizabeth Riley? Did you come to that conclusion yourself or did Kevin tell you that?"

I shook my head. What did Kevin have to do with this?! "No one told me that. Who else could it be!"

"Who else indeed."

Officer Randall's nonchalant attitude was really starting to piss me off. How often did skeletons turn up in the crawl spaces in Keyport?! "Well," Officer Randall mused, "if Elizabeth Riley is buried in the basement who killed Benjamin Riley?"

I looked at him dumbfounded. "I'm not a detective. I already found the body for you, why don't you figure out the rest." He didn't like that. I got the distinct feeling he was going to keep me out in the cold as long as he could. He flipped his notebook back to the beginning and started reading over his notes.

Something Jacklyn had said earlier that day ran through my mind. *I often think about how different my life would have turned out if he'd just let her go.'* "I don't know . . . maybe Benjamin killed Elizabeth because he caught her with her suitcase packed and couldn't let her go. After he murdered her, he felt guilty and took his own life."

Officer Randall rubbed his chin thoughtfully. "That sounds plausible. Good work, Morris."

Exacerbated, "Can I go home now?"

Officer Randall looked at his fellow officers crouched down near the crawl space window. "It looks like we're going to be here for a while. We don't have too many people who can fit into the crawl space," he said, patting his own stomach. "Probably why no one dug it up in the first place."

Officer Randall wasn't making Keyport feel like a safe place to live, but I wasn't going to be the one to break it to him.

"So that means I can go home then?"

"Yeah, go home," he finally said, as if he was thinking of asking me to go back under the crawl space but didn't have the authority. "If I need you, I'll call. Make sure you answer your phone."

* * *

By the time I got done with Officer Randall and made my way across the street to my house it was late. I remember it being past ten. The moon was tucked behind large clouds, and it was bitter cold out. The outside light was on, I assumed Liz flipped it on for me before she went to bed. I opened the front door to the sound of voices coming from the living room. One was Liz's, the other was very familiar to me. It only took a few seconds to place it as Jacklyn Riley's.

I'd forgotten to leave my coat in the car and was too lazy to walk back outside so I hung it on the hook on the back of the door. There was no way perfume could be detected over human sweat.

Hearing the front door open, my wife came bounding toward me like a lovesick puppy dog with Elizabeth Riley's teacup in her hands. I admit, I shouldn't have done what I did next, but I was exhausted, dirty, hungry, and most of all scared I was never going to get Liz back.

I grabbed her by her shoulders shaking her hard—way

harder than I should have. "I want my wife back!" I yelled at her; certain I was really talking to Elizabeth Riley.

"Morey you're hurting me," she whimpered, trying to break free of my grasp.

"I found your body; you should have peace now. Let my wife go!" I was sure I looked crazy in front of Jacklyn, but I didn't care. This had gone far enough. It had to end tonight.

"What are you talking about?!"

I wrestled the teacup from her like a madman. Scratch that, I was a madman. I completely lost it.

"Don't Morey!"

I threw it against the wall, it shattered.

Liz burst into tears. "How could you?"

Liz, my non-crier, was basically sobbing. I think I had only seen her cry once and that was when her childhood cat died. Seeing her cry now was more than I could take in my volatile state. I bit back my own tears. "I'm sorry Liz, I thought by breaking the teacup I would break the hold she had over you."

She wiped her tears with the back of her hand. "Her? What are you talking about?"

"I thought the ghost of Elizabeth Riley was somehow influencing you—maybe possessing you." I quickly offered my explanation. "I haven't had a chance to tell you yet, but I found her body today in the crawl space at Riley House." I looked to Jacklyn, assuming that was the very reason she was sitting in my living room, looking quite at home on my vintage couch. She must have driven to my home looking for me after I called her, wanting to talk or maybe wanting the teacup back that now lay shattered in pieces on the floor.

"I thought with the teacup gone things should go back to normal."

I stared at my wife hoping for a sign of my Liz—of the defiant artist I fell in love with.

"I think you need help," she said, wiping her eyeliner on the inside collar of her shirt. "You're the one who's been acting strangely. Since we moved here, you've been neurotic. You're really starting to scare me. If I didn't have Jackie to talk to, we wouldn't have made it this far. I'm going to my mom's until you cool off."

My eyes went to Jacklyn Riley. I suddenly felt ashamed and embarrassed for my behavior. I needed to justify my actions.

"I'm acting strange?!" I said indignantly. "You're the one painting creepy teacup portraits, listening to classical music, and cooking!" I knew it sounded crazy as I said it and Jacklyn's face confirmed it—I was crazy.

Oh God, was I the one that needed help? Was I the one possessed with my own crazy delusions? Was I having my very own *American Psycho* moment? I was glad I never brought home a kitten; I might have had the sudden urge to feed it through an ATM machine. But on the flipside, I would look really good running around the house naked with a chainsaw.

No—it's not me. I'm not the crazy one. The facts: Liz is acting weird, I found a body at Riley House that's most likely Elizabeth Riley's, and somehow the teacup led me to find it. The teacup marked the spot.

Liz shook her head at me like I was the biggest idiot she ever met. "I'm not possessed, I'm pregnant."

I took a step back, feeling every bit as crazy as she must have thought I was. The answer to all this, could it really be that simple?

"I'm listening to classical music because I read it will make the baby smarter. I'm cooking because I need to make sure I'm getting all the food groups. And I'm painting my portrait because when the baby comes, I want to paint a family portrait and there is no better way than to practice on yourself. And why the teacup, well it's also for practice," she said, glancing at Jacklyn on the couch. "Jackie has commissioned a series of teacups to be painted, and as you know, painting anything but landscapes are outside of my comfort zone, so I've been practicing."

My eyes darted back to Jacklyn Riley realizing she must be my wife's old friend Jackie that she caught up with since we moved to Keyport. I knew Jackie had started out as a client and over the years they had become friends, but I never met her. Did Jacklyn know who I was when she kissed me?

"Say something Morey," Liz said, breathlessly.

Relief and shame washed over me. And happiness, too. Liz and I hadn't talked about kids. "You're really pregnant?" Ignoring all the things I should apologize for, "Why didn't you tell me?"

"Yes," her expectant tone was of the Liz I love.

I hugged her, lifting her off the ground slightly. I kissed the top of her head, breathing in the fresh coconut smell.

Liz apologized to me. After everything I put her

through, it was she who apologized to me!

"I'm sorry, I didn't tell you right away. It was supposed to be your Christmas present. I shouldn't have kept it a secret. I see that now. The move has put too much pressure on you. I know it's not easy to commute like you do and you miss your family and the city, but I need you Morey. I need you to be in this when the baby comes."

"I will be. I promise," I said in a rushed voice. "I love you so much Liz. I'm not going anywhere."

I had forgotten Jacklyn Riley was still in our living room, that was until I heard her gun cock. I tried to push Liz out of the way, but it was too late. The bullet went through her then me, the force knocking us to the floor.

I was stunned not able to move at first. Gaining my awareness, I scrambled to Liz, the bullet pierced her shoulder. She was breathing but had been knocked unconscious by the bullet or the fall to the floor, I wasn't sure. I placed my hand over her wound, blood gushing over my fingertips. My own wound wasn't bad. I felt like the bullet just grazed the side of my chest.

I was so worried about Liz, I'd forgotten it was Jacklyn Riley who shot her and that she was still in the house.

"Pick her up," Jacklyn said, gesturing with her gun.

From my perch at the side of my wife, I looked up to see the barrel of a gun. It was still smoking from the last shot fired.

My thoughts were still on Liz. "She's pregnant! We have to get her to a hospital!"

"Pick her up," she said again, making sure to keep just

enough distance between us so I couldn't lunge at her without risking her shooting Liz or me. I needed time to think, to clear my head. I picked Liz up. She felt as light as a child in my arms.

Jacklyn led us into the basement, she was obviously very familiar with the layout of my house. She had me place Liz on the dirt floor. I tried to tear a piece of my shirt to wrap the bullet hole in Liz's shoulder, but to no avail—Under Armour doesn't tear.

Jacklyn marched me outside to her SUV to get a shovel. I glanced across the street at Riley House, hoping to spot Officer Randall. The digging at Riley House was happening on the side facing away from my home and Officer Randall wasn't near his car. There were, however, still police vehicles in the driveway. I could scream out for help or try to make a run for it, but if I did Jacklyn would shoot me. It would be worth it if I knew Officer Randall would hear me and come save Liz, but what if he didn't? What if no one heard me over the digging? Clearly no one heard the first shot and came running, despite I still had a ringing in my ears. I would be leaving Liz to be buried like Elizabeth had been buried. I wasn't going to risk that. I was going to save her.

I gripped the shovel, pain shooting across my palm from my earlier excavation. Jacklyn was smart. She was too far away from me to whack her with the shovel, but I just had to wait for her to make a mistake.

There was another problem. I was starting to think the bullet graze was more than a graze. My shirt was soaked with blood, and I was getting woozy.

I slowly made my way back down the attic steps waiting

for the opportunity to knock the grin off Jacklyn Riley's face. What did we ever do to her? Was this really over turning her down? I've had girls fight over me in the past, but this was insane.

I reached the bottom of the stairs, Jacklyn not giving me one moment to strike. Glancing to Liz, tears formed in the corners of my eyes. I held them back, I had to keep my composure if we were going to get out of this alive. I pawed at my face, Liz was still unconscious—so still she looked dead. I prayed she wasn't.

"Start digging," Jacklyn hissed at me.

"I'm sorry about what happened today. I am. I didn't mean to offend you. You're beautiful, it's just that I never had an affair before. Don't take the turn down personally, it had nothing to do with you and all with me."

That sounded good—really good, putting the blame on me would make all this go away. When that didn't work, I tried to appeal to her history with Liz. "You and Liz are friends. She's pregnant. You heard her. Help me do the right thing and let me take her to the hospital."

"I know; she told me. After all these years, you finally got her pregnant. Now dig, Benjamin."

Her calling me Benjamin again sent a shiver up my spine. I resisted the urge to shake it off like a wet dog. I was undoubtedly dealing with a woman who was mentally ill.

"Morris. My name is Morris Rossman." I glanced at my unconscious wife, "and she's Liz Rossman. I'll stay here with you, but please let her go Jackie."

Jacklyn's eyes darted around, making her look wholly

out of control. "You know I hate it when you call me that Benjamin, call me Jacklyn. I only ever let my Benji Kevin call me that."

That was it. Jacklyn Riley was nuts and she thought I was Benjamin Kevin Riley. Did that mean she thought Liz was Elizabeth?

Benji Kevin . . . Kevin? I'd just realized that my neighbor Kevin Riley was Benjamin Kevin Riley. It hit me like a ton of bricks, wobbling me. That's why Officer Randall didn't take my police report seriously, he knew Kevin was dead.

Sarah at the historical society had alluded to it, saying she hoped Kevin could leave Riley House behind him, and had given me his new address—the address to Keyport Cemetery. Jacklyn had also claimed to have seen Benjamin's ghost, even if it was only once, noting the townsfolk had made the same claim.

I was beyond frustrated with myself that I didn't put it together before now. If I had, maybe I could have let it all go. Liz wasn't possessed, she was pregnant. I let superstition get the best of me. In fairness, I was partially right, something otherworldly was going on. But it had nothing to do with Liz and so it shouldn't have mattered to me, and I'm certain it wouldn't have. Kevin could keep on moving teacups in Riley House for eternity and Elizabeth, though it pained me to think it, could have stayed buried with her secrets. None of this was worth losing Liz.

I cursed myself for the second time that day. I'd even seen Kevin in the cemetery standing in front of Benjamin Kevin Riley's grave—his new home by the water, close to family. He'd seemed to vanish when I turned my back. How could I have been so blind—so stupid. This was all about Benjamin, helping Benjamin get peace for his wife. I don't know why he couldn't just have told Officer Randall, but how did Jacklyn fit into this? Kevin had mentioned a son not a daughter.

My current predicament and inquisitive nature answered that for me. I had a horrible feeling. I was sure I knew exactly how Jacklyn fit into this puzzle, but I needed to hear it from her.

I played the part of Benjamin Riley. At this point, I was pretty sure she was convinced I was him anyway. I just hoped my acting skills, as bad as they were, could keep her in the moment. "Why Jacklyn? Why'd you do it? We took you in."

As if on cue, "I did it for you. I loved you. You know how much I love you."

Her consciousness seemed to go back and forth, recognizing me as Benjamin one moment and the next moment as myself—her verbiage switching from the past to the present, to only slip back into the past. I took the opportunity to rest, leaning my weight on the shovel. The basement floor was proving harder to dig up than I would've expected. It was as hard as stone. Digging even a shallow grave was going to take forever. Was this a stroke of good luck or was my strength failing me? I could feel blood trickling down my leg and that alarmed me. I was cold—very cold. The basement was a good ten degrees cooler than the rest of the house, but the cold sweat that broke out across my forehead couldn't have been a good sign. I tried to conserve my energy by taking slow, meaningful breaths that stung my lungs.

"Benjamin and Elizabeth Riley adopted me at the age of ten. The years flew by, and I matured quickly. Benjamin, when he thought no one was looking, would steal glances at me. It wasn't long until we fell in love. He was ready to apply for a divorce when Elizabeth got pregnant. That stupid, stupid woman ruined everything. They had been married for almost a decade and she'd never conceived. Just when I was about to get everything I ever wanted, she became pregnant with a son. A legitimate son. He said that to me over and over again. Said his son was legitimate.

"It was all set. Benjamin was giving her half of his fortune, and I was getting him, but he wouldn't leave her after that. He said we had to stop seeing each other romantically and go back to a father daughter relationship, but I couldn't. I thought if I could just get rid of Elizabeth it would fix everything.

"It was me who started the rumors she was cheating on him with Bill Blair next door. Bill had a reputation as a womanizer and it was no secret Bill, along with lots of men in town, fancied Elizabeth. I hoped the rumors would get back to Benjamin and he would doubt the legitimacy of his son and leave her. But still he wouldn't let her go. Not even with the whole town whispering behind his back.

"My Benji Kevin became suspicious of me. He started to treat me like a stepchild, even threatened to send me away. I did what I had to do," Jacklyn said in a tone that made me feel like this was it for Liz and me. I didn't doubt she would do anything she had to do to get what she wanted. If only there was a way to get her to stay in the present and force her to realize I was not her ex-lover.

Stupefied, it struck me she was in the present. She was telling me the story of her and Benjiman Riley like I was me, Morris Rossman, the guy she met for the first time today. Why hadn't she come to her senses and realized digging a shallow grave for her friend and her husband in their basement wasn't a good idea?!

"Every day after school I would crawl into the crawl space and dig for a couple hours until I had dug Elizabeth's grave. I drugged my stepmother and dragged her into the crawl space when Benjamin was at work. Then I went into her room and packed her suitcase, burying it with her.

"As soon as Benjamin got home that night, I told him she'd left with another man, and we could finally be together in the way we had always hoped. I thought he'd be happy she was gone, but he was so fixated on his son. He vowed to spend his fortune to find her and bring her back."

She looked to me for empathy, waving her gun at me to make sure I was listening. "Can you imagine how that made me feel?! Can you imagine what it was like for me when he told me our affair was a mistake? That he should never have adopted me! That he loved Elizabeth and his unborn child more than he will ever love me!"

Her tone deepened, "Dig!" I spurred into motion.

"Benjamin was going to be sorry. He was going to be very sorry. That night I agreed to let my childish dreams go and be just his daughter. I told him I would do what I could to help bring Elizabeth and my brother home.

"That night after dinner, I made him his cup of tea as I always did but served it in Elizabeth's favorite teacup. He, just like you, questioned why she would leave the teacup behind. By the time he realized she didn't leave it behind by choice, it was too late. He was dying in my arms, and I told him what I did to his precious Elizabeth and son."

I was speechless. That was the holy shit of confessions. At the risk of another outburst, I leaned against my shovel for support, taking in the crazy.

My cell phone went off. Jacklyn shook her head. I ignored it and continued to dig.

The opening line to Charles Dickens's *David Copperfield* popped into my head: 'Whether I shall turn out to be the hero of my own life, or whether that station will be held by anybody else, these pages must show.' I so wanted to be the hero. I wanted to save Liz and the baby, but I was running out of time. The smell of my own blood mingled with the earthy smells of damp soil was becoming too much for me. I was pretty sure I would pass out from blood loss before I finished digging. Keyport Cemetery suddenly seemed like a nice place to end up. Anything would be better than this basement.

I glanced at Liz. I wanted to check on her but didn't want to draw Jacklyn's attention in her direction.

I did all I could in my situation. If Jacklyn wanted empathy, I'd give it to her. "Jacklyn, I'm sorry Benjamin hurt you. You were a child, and he took advantage of your situation. There's no need to go through with this. What you did to Elizabeth and Benjamin could be seen as a crime of passion.

They let people off for that all the time. But what you're doing here with Liz and me is murder. It's not too late to stop this. Think about it, Liz is pregnant. You don't want that on your conscience." I paused, the image of Elizabeth in her wedding dress popping into my mind's eye. She too was pregnant and that didn't stop Jacklyn from dragging her into the crawl space. "Let me call an ambulance for Liz and I promise not to say a word about Benjamin and Elizabeth Riley. I will tell Officer Randall what happened to Liz was an accident. Please Jacklyn."

Jacklyn smiled, flashing her bright teeth at me like a lit jack o' lantern. "Tonight is about finishing what I started."

I groaned; we were back to that. "I'm not Benjamin Riley!"

"No, you're not. You're Morris Rossman Riley. You're the spitting image of your grandfather."

"You're mistaken," I said, the shovel becoming increasingly heavy in my hands. "I'm adopted. I don't know who my biological father is. So, there's no knowing who my grandfather was. And besides, you already confessed to burying Elizabeth and her unborn child in the crawl space."

Jacklyn's eyes were alive with madness. "I delivered Benjamin's son before I buried Elizabeth. I cut out the baby while his mother still breathed. Once the baby was free of her, I walked to the police station, leaving him on their doorstep. I was going to surprise Benjamin with his son. I'd planned on telling him that Elizabeth confided in me that she had delivered early and left his son at the Keyport Police Station for him. That in doing this, she hoped he would not follow her as she started her new life without him.

"That was before he ruined everything by denouncing me. After I took care of Beth and Benjamin Kevin, I went back for the baby. By then, the baby had been taken to the hospital. I was still a minor, not having the Riley resources at my fingertips to procure the baby. The baby was adopted and he, along with his new family, moved. I didn't get a chance to kill your biological father, but I *will* kill you." She glanced at Liz. "And end the Riley bloodline."

There it was—the why. She had come to her senses. Maybe she was a little senile, but she knew exactly what she was doing and to whom. I was dumbstruck. I had noticed the similarities between Benjamin and myself in his wedding photo. Kevin was older than me and had a beard, but now that I knew the truth, I saw it.

"When you showed up at my doorstep, I couldn't believe it. It was as if Benji Kevin came back from the dead. Every detail of your face reminds me of him. You have the same eyes, chin, and hair before he went gray, even the same dimples. It wasn't difficult to find out you were adopted and trace you back to Benjamin. And then to find out you were Liz's husband—all my ducks lined up in a row.

I groaned. I would never use that colloquialism again to describe my uptightness, even if I didn't have that much time left.

Jacklyn aimed the gun at my chest. "So once again history repeats itself. Another Riley chooses his pregnant wife over me."

I put my hands up innocently, the shovel falling to the ground.

I felt lightheaded from the blood loss; sick—a wave of nausea washing over me as I fought the urge to vomit. "I can't believe this is how I'm going to die," I said over and over again as if repeating this mantra would somehow save my life. The repetition of words at the very least gave me something to focus on besides dying. Somehow the idea of being discovered murdered, lying in my own throw up, would make my death just that more indignant, that much harder for me to accept.

A knock sounded on the front door. "Police!"

Jacklyn looked toward the stairs. I seized the moment, grabbing the shovel and swinging with all the strength I had left. The gun went off. The bullet struck my shoulder, forcing me to drop the shovel and sending me whirling back. I was able to steady myself enough to reverse the direction of my fall, lunging for Jacklyn's feet just as she fired another shot. I tackled her to the ground, wrestling the gun from her. Officer Randall ran down the basement steps to the sound of the gun shots.

"Call an ambulance," I yelled, pinning Jacklyn to the ground.

CHAPTER TEN
The New Beginning

I unpacked the box labeled 'kitchen' in our new home. It felt right to be back in the city in a high-rise apartment. I was glad things were finally getting back to normal. My shoulder was still a little sore, but it too was almost back to normal. The important thing was the past was behind us. Jacklyn Riley was in jail. Her trial was next month. We wouldn't be seeing her again, and I was about to inherit the Riley fortune. It made taking a loss on the sale of Billandbeth easier to handle. Taking real estate losses is not something realtors take lightly. Keyport would always be a blemish on my perfect portfolio, but I didn't care. It didn't matter to me that months later the office was still having a laugh at my expense. They weren't there. They didn't live through what Liz and I did.

Liz and I just wanted the last months of her pregnancy to be peaceful and that meant putting Keyport behind us. Well not completely. We'd decided to name the baby Benjamin after my grandfather. In acknowledging my family's history, we hoped history wouldn't repeat itself.

I wasn't crazy about naming the baby Benjamin, even though ironically that was my own middle name, but it was between that or Randall after Officer Randall who saved our lives.

When I didn't answer my phone, Officer Randall decided to knock on my door since I lived literally across the street to tell me he needed me to come to the police station in the morning to make an official statement. Officer Randall had seen the blood from my bullet wound in the driveway and on the steps leading to my house and barged in, giving me the distraction I needed to get the gun away from Jacklyn. I grudgingly liked the name Benjamin better than Randall. I guess things have a funny way of working out.

As for Benjamin and Elizabeth Riley, I hope that now that justice has been served and Beth was put to rest next to her husband, she and Kevin could both find peace.

I unwrapped the last mug from the box. It wasn't a coffee mug. It should have been a coffee mug. One of a matching set, but in my hands, I held a bone-china teacup with roses painted on it. I examined the teacup with a wary eye. It was the same one I shattered against my living room wall back in Keyport. I was sure of it. I could see faint cracks where it had broken, but the surface was smooth as if the cracks were a deliberate part of the glazing. I turned the teacup upside down to read Liz Riley.

I heard my wife come up behind me. "Would you like a cup of tea?"

I turned around to see Liz's eyes glinting like green cat eyes. She'd dyed her hair blonde. Her smile curled to the side just as it did in the portrait she had painted in Keyport.

"Liz, what did you do to your hair?" I asked, almost dropping the teacup. She took it from me. "Careful cu-tea you almost broke my favorite teacup and it's Beth now. Never kettle for second best."

The End . . .

THANKS FOR READING!

If this book helped you escape, if only for a moment, please consider taking the time to leave a review or star rating on Amazon or whatever platform you use. It would warm the cockles of my little, black heart to hear from you.

Looking for something else to read? Don't forget to check out my other books on Amazon.

Follow me on social media (I'm on all platforms under Holly Knightley). Sign up for my newsletter for the latest news, glimpse into my wacky process, and occasional freebie. Stay spooky and happy reading!

WANT MORE?

THE KILLING TREE

CHAPTER ONE

The Confession

Hitch came into our dorm room frantic. He did that from time to time and I didn't pay much attention. He was a film major, to which he said he had no choice in the matter. The stars foretold his greatness, owing to the fact he was born under the last name Hitchcock. He always said his mother did him a great injustice not naming him after the famous film director Alfred Hitchcock. He commented ad nauseam how great it would be to be called Alfred Hitchcock II versus Charles Alphonse Hitchcock. He settled for Charlie Hitch and was known simply as Hitch to his closest friends.

Hitch rushed to his oversize safe at the foot of his bed. He turned the combination as if he was defusing a bomb. It housed his blue binder that contained all of his movie ideas, scripts, trade secrets, and probably a key to another dimension. Before the mammoth safe, the binder was tucked under his bed. That was until his paranoia got the best of him and he sprang for the safe. On more than a few occasions some of his film buddies would attempt to break into it or move it to mess with him, but to no avail. Hitch's blue binder would survive an atomic bomb.

After thumbing through his binder in genuine concentration,

with beads of sweat dripping from his furrowed brow, he threw it on the floor. With a dramatic freefall that produced a groan that made it sound like we may have seen the last of his bed, he outstretched his arms to an invisible god. "Why?! Why have you forsaken me!"

"Everything okay Hitch?" I asked from my desk where I was busy working on Chemistry IV equations for my final exam that Friday.

"No! Life as I know it is over. *The Stranger*'s been slashed."

"Slashed as in shelved?" I asked, trying to keep up.

The Stranger was his senior film project he'd been working on since the beginning of the semester. He spent every waking moment either working on it or talking about it. It had dawned on me long ago, I could've gotten a minor in film just from his secondhand knowledge. That might have looked really good on my medical school applications, but it didn't matter, I'd already attained early acceptance to Stanford Medical for next fall.

"Yes, shelved. The old girl has been put where all films go to die."

"It can't be that bad," I assured him, not looking up from my study guide. "You loved it last week. I'm sure whatever it is you don't like now can be fixed in edits."

I felt his eyes boring holes into my back. I turned around to face him. His eyes looked like storm clouds; they were calling for rain. Maybe it *was* that bad.

"It's bad. Jill's the worst actress in the history of the world! Directing is good, the story is good, but the acting . . . the acting is shit!"

I held back my comment about the director directing the actors. "Can't you just reshoot Jill's scenes?"

"Oh Knox, you have all the answers, don't you?!" He placed his pillow over his face and screamed into it.

I knew cutting Jill from *The Stranger* was out of the question. Jill was Hitch's girlfriend and if she didn't have that title, at the very least, she was his good friend with benefits. Though I was convinced one day Hitch would be big in the movie industry and have starlets on his arms everywhere he went, right now he was the closest thing to a real-life girl repellent I'd ever seen. For as fun as Hitch is, he's just as unattractive. Like his idol, he's husky with a nose that resembles a beak. To complete his look, he shaves his red hair, showing the world a shiny scalp that could serve as a makeshift mirror.

I didn't agree, but Hitch was convinced I could play a heartthrob if I ditched the glasses and what he dubbed 'the science stuff,' not that I wore a pocket protector or anything. It was true, I'd filled out since high school and was no longer short and scrawny, but a heartthrob I was not.

After what happened with Evelyn Butler in high school, I couldn't talk to girls without my mouth getting dry and my palms beading up with sweat. I was pretty sure everyone at school thought I had a glandular problem. I essentially assigned myself to die a virgin and had come to terms with that.

"It's not only Jill," Hitch said, removing the pillow from half of his face and fixating on me with his exposed eye. "The Stranger, the actual person, as in the killer, is awful! If there was someone in charge of casting, I'd fire them." He moaned into the pillow, "I don't get it. Gerald was so good at tryouts! As soon as the camera cuts to him, he freezes up."

Hitch tossed aside the pillow and propped himself up on his elbows. "You know what, you could play the killer. You'd be perfect! You already have all the creepy mannerisms down. You'd be like another Ted Bundy."

I turned away from Hitch and went back to studying. Two people couldn't be more different. I was very quiet, to the point of strange, but I wouldn't call my mannerisms creepy. Freshman year, Hitch probably would've traded rooms with someone the first chance he got if it weren't for my name, or more precisely my last name which I share with the late actress Angela Lansbury. He took it as a sign. Just as the stars had laid out his favorable fate in Hollywood, they foretold our everlasting friendship. Roommates both having Hollywood royalty surnames had to mean something.

Hitch pulled himself from his bed and hovered by my desk. "What you say buddy ole' pal, will you do it?"

"I don't appreciate being compared to a serial killer."

"I wasn't comparing you, not really. And being the next Ted Bundy wouldn't be a bad thing. He did get all the ladies, if only to kill them. Besides, it's just a movie."

I didn't respond.

He put his hand to his forehead and pretended to faint. "It's not always about you Knox Lansbury. This is my life. You think as my best friend you'd help me out. Let's reshoot with you as the killer?"

I shook my head without looking up.

"Please."

"No," I said, not entertaining it.

He laced his fingers together as if in prayer. "Pretty please? I'll even let you wear your glasses."

He pulled my glasses off to examine them. "These may give off a glare in some scenes. We may have to visit the props department."

I snatched back my glasses, "I said no."

Again, he threw himself onto his bed. A horrible squeaking noise pursued as he rocked himself back and forth like he was strapped into a straitjacket. The noise made the muscles in my back tense. "Why not? Give me one good reason. We both know you don't have to study."

Heat rushed to my face and cheeks, ultimately reaching the tips of my ears. I had held my secret so close for so long, I suppose sooner or later it had to come out. Secrets like mine always do. Ted Bundy's did.

"What is it?" Hitch asked, no doubt noticing the color change in my complexion. I was unvaryingly even mannered; not letting things get to me. I preferred it that way, to fly under the radar and blend into my surroundings like a chameleon. Maybe I *would* be a good actor . . . or good serial killer for that matter.

I trusted Hitch more than anyone in the world. He had long ago become my best friend. And there was this part of me that wanted to tell someone, and a smaller part that wanted to tell everyone. "Hitch I can't play a killer because . . ."

"Because?"

It was now, or never. If I wanted to get it off my chest, this was my chance. I shut my textbook and looked Hitch dead in the eyes, his blue eyes twinkling with hope. "I can't play a killer because *I am* a killer . . . It's all just to real for me."

I let my back conform to my seat as my shoulders sagged forward. It was finally out. My dark secret had come to see the light of day.

I deserved every reprehensible thought Hitch could think upon hearing such a confession. It couldn't be worse than my own nocturnal condemnations. Murder is wrong. It's the most loathsome of human behavior. In fact, it's not human at all—it's animalistic. We, as a species, have evolved above this basic 'fight to live' principle that Charles Darwin outlined in *The Origin of Species.* Being human defies the scientific principle of survival of the fittest.

Hitch snorted a high pitch laugh. It wasn't his normal laugh; it was sprinkled with anxiety as if part of him believed I *could* be a killer.

"You're pulling my leg," he said, a smile tugging at the corners of his lips until he was grinning like the Cheshire Cat. He always did that, smiled ear to ear when he was particularly proud of something he said and always when he used a line he would consider to be 'in the business.' "I see what's happening here, Gerald knew he was on the chopping block and asked you to say no. Knox, you're a better actor than I thought. You *have to* play the part now!"

I shook my head, trying to make my point. "Gerald didn't put me up to it. I murdered my brother."

His shoulders slumped, his double chin now resting on his chest. "You told me a tree fell on him."

"Both are true."

He disingenuously acted intrigued, sitting tall in his bed. "Let me guess, you pushed it on him. Wait, no, you lured him there divining it was going to fall. Or the most likely, you drugged him, then placed him under the tree, then timber!"

"It didn't happen like that."

"How *did* it happen?" he asked incredulously.

Returning to my study guide, "Forget it."

My entire face felt like it was on fire. My heart pounded in my chest as it reverberated in my ears. I regretted opening my mouth. Telling Hitch my secret didn't make me feel any better, if anything I felt worse. Admitting to Lincoln's murder out loud made me feel like a killer. I was, I knew that. How could I ever forget, but to feel it take a hold of me again made me lightheaded.

"Knox tell me," Hitch nagged, his voice taking on a high-pitched tone. "You can't say something like that and not elaborate."

"I can't tell you the truth, you'd never believe me."

He let out a noise that rivaled a rhinoceros at the zoo.

"I can't tell you, but I can show you."